Ricky

RICKY

J. Boyett

SALTIMBANQUE BOOKS

NEW YORK

For Pam Carter, Dawn Drinkwater, and Andy Shanks.

Also for Ron Kolm, whether he likes it or not.

Ricky

1.

There were cigarette butts in the parking lot and littering the pavement before her door. It pissed Ricky off that his little sister had to put up with this after she'd worked so hard and come so far, at least by their family's standards. Elly shrugged and tried to shush him: "I don't mind," she said.

"Well, I mind for you."

"There are so many more important problems." She sounded weary, so Ricky shut up. He was trying not to get on her nerves.

She showed him around the apartment. Since she could afford it he thought she should move out to pricier, more prestigious west Little Rock, but she explained that this area down by the river had more character; Ricky instantly submitted to her judgment. He gaped at the beige carpet, afraid to walk on it. The walls were clean. There was a flat-screen TV mounted on the wall, which he stared at a while before he understood what it was doing there. He gingerly tested the sofa's resistance with one hand: "Did you buy this *new?*"

Elly seemed uneasy. She must have imagined this as a kind of homecoming for him, and it obviously didn't feel like home if he was so shocked at having been allowed to come in the front door. "You want a beer?" she said as she disappeared into the kitchen. "I remember in your letters you always talked about how much you wished you could have beer in jail."

"Sure, thanks," said Ricky, and then, "I said that? I don't guess I was such a good role model."

Elly came back with two open Sam Adamses and handed him one, her head tilted back to look up at him. "I wasn't exactly a little girl when you went in," Elly said, and then took a swig off her own bottle.

Ricky blushed. "No, I know that."

They stood there together a few seconds, facing each other, both trying not to look away. Finally, Elly said, "I think it's fine that it'll be awkward for the first couple of days. I don't think that means anything bad."

"No, yeah, me too," said Ricky hurriedly. Then he said, "I feel in one way like we should get caught back up, but then it's like I already know everything from your letters."

Elly laughed and said, "God, I know, I'm sorry. All those years of babbling to you on and on about nothing."

"No. Those letters meant a lot to me, Elly."

"Yeah, right. Tall tales and gossip. It was nice of you to not tell me to quit bugging you. All my silly little dramas."

"I'm being for real, Elly. I loved your stories. I would have wished I was dead if I hadn't been hearing from you like that."

"You want to watch TV?" she asked. Ricky nodded, desperate as he was to lay the weight of his gratitude before her. After all she'd done he had no business forcing her to take it if she didn't want to. She went to get the remote from the end table: "You're going to freak out when you see how many channels there are on digital cable. There're hundreds, literally. It's weird the things that've changed since you went away."

"They say the world's changing really fast."

The TV came on noisily but for the first few seconds Ricky just kept looking at Elly. She seemed dressed-up to him: black slacks, jacket, white blouse, a plain silver bracelet, a pearl necklace (wowed as he was, Ricky knew they weren't real pearls); he watched as she took off her jacket and carefully hung it up in the hall closet. She sat down on the sofa, noticed that he was still staring at her instead of the television, got uncomfortable again, and said, "You want to pick the channel? I'll have to teach you how to work the remote. They're more complicated now."

Ricky walked around to the front of the couch. Elly had sat on the far right cushion. Should he plant himself in the

4

middle cushion so he'd be sitting close to her, or would it be more natural to sit on the far side, the way she'd done? After hesitating, he sat beside her, on the middle cushion. She didn't seem to mind.

She held the remote out towards him. "You want to choose the channel?" she said again.

"Nah, that's okay, you go ahead."

"You sure?" she pressed; it seemed important to her. "It's been so long since you've gotten to do it, I bet."

That was true. There'd been TV in prison, of course, but he'd never been the one to pick the programming. Even if him taking the remote control was something that Elly truly wanted, he didn't have it in him right now to try to figure the thing out: there were so many buttons on it. "No, it's cool, I'd rather you do it," he said, stopping himself from adding, "It's your TV."

She flipped channels and showed him the menu functions. He made appreciative noises and didn't tell her that they'd had digital cable in prison and none of this was as new to him as she thought. She found one of her favorite shows, explained its storyline. He listened dutifully. Then they settled in to watch.

After a long time of not talking, Ricky mustered himself and turned to Elly's profile. "Hey, Elly," he said. "There's something I need to tell you."

Elly turned to him, not quickly, looking prepared but not thrilled; "Sure," she said, "tell me anything you want."

"I always wanted to tell you. I always felt like I was lying to you. And I guess I was, and I'm sorry. But I couldn't have told you in a letter."

There was half a second where everything was frozen. Elly said, "Go ahead. I love you, you can tell me anything."

"Elly. The truth is I wasn't just the driver. I did shoot one of them. With the gun that Steve threw into the lake afterwards. I only shot one, but still."

Elly's eyes teared up, but she smiled at him. "Yeah, I figured," she said, "I just always kind of figured."

Ricky didn't say anything.

"I used to think to myself, Thank God the cops shot everyone else but Ricky. It scared me to think that—I mean, Steve was the only one of the guys I knew, but I always did like him. I even had sort of a crush on him I guess. And the other guys, I mean, I knew they were *your* friends. But even so, I used to always think, Thank God they all got shot. So that there'd be nobody to argue when the lawyers said that Ricky hadn't done anything."

Ricky felt like now he should admit that he'd often thought the same thing himself, about his own friends, but he didn't. He said, "Your letters always meant so much to me, I loved getting your letters and hearing all your stories. I can't wait to meet all these people you've told me about, to meet Paul, and—"

"Paul and I broke up. Four months ago."

"I know that—"

"Now it's Ted, the thug...." Elly cut herself off at the word "thug," grimaced, glanced from under her eyebrows at Ricky. "Sorry," she said.

Ricky was mortified that she thought he'd forgotten that she'd broken up with Paul. "I know all that. I just meant...." He trailed off, unable to think of how to express the truth, which was that he'd gotten accustomed to thinking of Paul and the rest of them as a cast of characters rather than as real people. He knew that Paul had dicked over his little sister, but he still had a certain detached curiosity about the guy. But if that ambiguity was ever going to be talked about (which was hard to imagine) it would be best if it happened some other time. So Ricky kept his mouth shut, since his constant apologizing was getting on his own nerves, and probably Elly's too, and "Sorry" was the only thing he could think of to say.

They watched TV. Suddenly Ricky was in a really foul mood. He fantasized about beating the shit out of Paul, a guy he'd never met, lovingly imagined kicking him until he turned into a jelly-bag: not just how it would look, but the tactile stuff, and the sounds, he tried to imagine what the smells would be, the way his shins would start to hurt, the way he'd be risking a twisted ankle. The weird thing was that, whereas in all these ways the fantasy was vivid and concrete, the fact that he'd never met Paul or even seen his picture meant that where the human should be there was only a vague phantom, an identity that didn't quite consent to slip out from behind whatever it was ducked on the other side of. He could feel his breathing getting harder, and probably Elly could hear the change—he forced himself to calm down.

Elly patted his knee. "I'm so happy you're back," she said again.

"Me too," said Ricky, and then sort of laughed, because of course he was.

Then he realized that she was crying. When she saw that he knew, she leaned in to hide her snuffling face in his chest. He gripped her tight, cupping the back of her skull in his palm. "Shhh, shhh," he said.

She reached up her arms to hug him back. Her fingers gripped the nape of his neck. Ricky put his arms around her waist, rubbed her back.

She raised her head, put her mouth on his without looking at his face. Ricky didn't exactly kiss her back, but he didn't stop her from nudging his lips apart with hers, from inserting the very tip of her tongue into his mouth, where it didn't really do anything except tremble in uncertainty and hesitation.

He pulled his head back. "Whoa," he said, "whoa, whoa."

Elly pulled back, didn't look straight at him, gazed into the distance dead-eyed and sullen.

Ricky was breathing really hard, now. He caught his breath, cleared his throat, said, "We can't do that anymore, Elly."

Elly was looking at the TV. "Yeah," she said, "of course," as if he'd brought the subject up out of the blue. She didn't look away from the TV.

They sat in silence for a while. "Well, I better take off," Ricky said, at the same time that he got to his feet. The effort required to get out of this super-soft couch surprised him.

Elly looked up at him, not getting to her feet during these

7

first few seconds, her expression alarmed, guilty, scared. "You sure?" she said.

"Yeah. It's just going to take time for me to get used to it, I think. Being around people. Baby steps, you know."

"Yeah?" Then he could see her mentally shaking herself, trying not to be sentimental, to be a grown-up. "Of course," she said, standing up. "It's a big adjustment."

She walked him to the door, and patted him on the back encouragingly. Thinking of the way she'd kissed him, nuzzling his lips apart, he started to cry. Elly squeezed his upper arm with one hand, put her other arm around his shoulder. "Hey," she encouraged. "That's okay. Go ahead, if you need to."

Ricky was shaking his head. "I'm sorry," he said.

"For what?" she said, but sounded nervous. But maybe that was only his imagination.

He kept shaking his head. "I haven't been a very good brother to you," was the closest he could come up with.

"No," she said, firmly, rallying herself. "Hey now. No. You hear? I don't want to hear that kind of stuff."

"It's true," said Ricky, trying to stop crying so that they could stop talking about why he was crying.

"No it isn't," she insisted, then, to lighten things up, said, "You're my favorite brother."

The joke being that he was her only brother, her only sibling. The polite thing would have been to acknowledge the gag with a wry smile and a headshake. He did shake his head, but he didn't smile and all he said was, "It's true."

"Hey." Now, as a woman taking care of a man, Elly was in her element. She clenched both his shoulders in her hands, repositioning herself so that they faced each other. "Hey," she said, "you listen to me, okay now? You just listen to me. Now, I want you to forgive yourself. You hear? That's the only thing I want."

Ricky was still sniffling, but he was basically back under control now, which meant that soon he'd be free to go. He shook his head again and said, "You shouldn't want that."

"But I do," said Elly, now adopting the tone you'd use with a child to signal that though you sympathize with it, it nevertheless amuses you. "I do want it. You're my brother and I love you. And whatever you think you've done wrong by me, or even whatever you really *have* done wrong by me, I just want you to forgive yourself for it."

Ricky had stopped crying. He looked at Elly and said, "Yeah, but you only want that because you're fucked up."

Her face froze. "What?" she said.

"You're fucked up. That's why you think I didn't do anything wrong, is because you're all fucked up. Because I fucked you up. Me."

Elly kept staring at him. "Jesus Christ," she said. "Did I say that you didn't do anything wrong?"

They stood there for many seconds. Then Elly said, "I guess you'd better go, after all."

Ricky bowed his head, submissively, nodded it. "Yeah."

"No," Elly said hurriedly, "I didn't mean that. Or, I mean, I did, but. . . ." She floundered, then gave up. "I only meant it the literal way," she finally settled for, giving him a tired smile that also felt like a request.

He smiled back. "Okay," he said. He tried to appear sure on his feet.

At the front door they looked at each other again, waiting for something. "It'll just take a while," Ricky reassured her.

"Yeah," she quickly agreed. "I know. I don't think it's a big deal. I think it's okay if we give ourselves permission to just, you know, screw up a little in the beginning."

"Totally," he said, trying not to notice what a brave face she was putting on her disappointment. And it wasn't just for the sake of her pride, or dignity, that he tried not to notice. They stood there another four or five seconds. Then Ricky shrugged and said, "Well."

"Yeah, well," said Elly. They embraced each other again. She gave him a squeeze and said, "I've been looking forward to this day more than anything for years now." As they stepped

9

apart she gave an embarrassed laugh, and he knew that she'd said that only because she'd been rehearsing the line for so long, that having planned it for so many years had turned it into an obligation.

"Me, too," he said. They had to hug each other again once the door was opened. Then, as he walked to the car their mother had loaned him, he had to turn to look at her over his shoulder and wave. She waved back. Then once he was in the car and driving out of the parking lot he had to look again and they had to wave again to each other. It was a relief when he rounded the corner of the building and she was gone from view. But it wasn't that he didn't want to see her; in fact the sight was precious. What he wished was that he might be invisible, so that he could look at her, but without her seeing him do it, so that he would not have to worry about how to arrange his gaze, about the things she might see in it or think she saw in it, that might or might not really be there at all, so that it might be as if he and his gaze didn't exist at all, but only her and the fact of the sight of her.

2.

He ought to have gone home to his mother, she deserved to see him too. But all the obligations were getting to him, and it seemed like since he'd gone away to jail she had gotten tough enough to stand his absence.

Besides, he reminded himself, his state of mind could do with some looking-after, too. He had just been released this morning from prison after being there for nearly a decade. But when he tried to remind himself of this, to give himself permission to worry about his own psyche, he got hung up on the fact that he'd deserved all the bad things that had happened to him (he'd deserved worse).

As for the awkwardness that he felt around his sister, that shouldn't have been a surprise. Every time he'd seen her since going away, they'd had the ritual of the prison visitation process there, to structure and sustain them. And the enjoyment he had always gotten from the stories she regaled him with in her letters might not be the kind of thing that could be transmitted by mere everyday conversation.

He might not want to go to his mom's house, off shitty Baseline Road in south Little Rock, but that didn't mean he had anywhere else to go. There were some places in town that stuck out in his memory. But he wasn't ready to see the people who would be there. It hadn't yet occurred to him that the old haunts would be mostly emptied of the buddies he'd known, replaced with a new generation; nor had it struck him yet that those guys, even if he did run into them again, would no longer be teenagers. All of them would have the beginnings of crows' feet, some would be going bald. He was still imagining these reunions as super-emotional, it hadn't occurred to him that they wouldn't mainly involve exclamations and back-clapping embraces. No one else was going to be able to muster the fake emotion necessary, any more than he could.

But he did have to go somewhere, he couldn't just drive aimlessly all over Little Rock, although actually he did do that for a while. Finally he headed downtown, towards what in his time had been a seedy district and he supposed still was: crackhouses, homeless people, the Capitol building. Also Vino's, the pizza place and punk venue. As he pulled off onto the freeway exit, it occurred to him that Vino's might have closed down after all these years. He didn't know what he would do if Vino's was gone.

It was still there. He pulled into its moonscape of a parking lot, crawling along so as to avoid scraping the undercarriage of his mom's car against the epic potholes. Then he dawdled while locking the car, gazing around at the buildings. Vino's looked shockingly the same. In the windows were all sorts of unlit neon signs which he had forgotten about but which he recognized now.

The interior was similarly weird, the shock of all these prosaic details that had bothered to continue existing even though it had never occurred to him to bother recalling them. At the same time, none of the people he had invested the power of his memory in were there, their important positions filled by bit players, as if the blockbuster movie of his childhood had been adapted into a television show with the same set but unknown actors. There were a couple of faces he recognized, though, and it was an ugly shock to see how they'd aged. Part of him felt obliged to say hello to them, to explain that he'd just gotten out of prison. But these punk-scene lifers all happened to be guys he hadn't thought about in years, whose names he couldn't remember, and he couldn't walk up and tell them something like that if he couldn't even call them by their names.

At Vino's, you lined up at the counter to place your order and pay in advance. Ricky hesitated before getting in line as if there were some chance that he might do it wrong.

He wasn't in the line very long before he noticed there was a cute girl at the head of it, taking orders. It had been years since he'd touched a woman, except for Elly earlier, and his horniness had reached a painful peak in the days before his release, but today's drama had drowned out those feelings. But at the sight of the chipmunk-cheeked girl behind the counter, a hard-on asserted itself with such force that he would have been embarrassed to keep standing, if he hadn't been so distracted.

His turn came. He stood there a long time without saying anything, staring at the girl, feeling stupid. She took it in stride, leaning against the counter, her arms outstretched as she braced herself against her palms, surveying him with her small dark eyes, her head cocked, her mouth neither firm nor lax. She didn't deign to snap him out of his dumb reverie; finally the guy behind Ricky said, "Uh, dude?" Ricky said, "What beer's good?"

The girl shrugged. "We have a microbrewery. That's pretty good. I mean, it's fresh, we make it here."

"Okay. I'll have that. A pint. And a slice of pizza."

"What kind?"

Ricky gaped, said, "What pizza's good?"

Now she smiled for him. "A lesser man would've just said cheese."

"I'm not a lesser man."

She rolled her eyes, but didn't stop smiling. "The Supreme's good," she said.

"I'll have a slice of Supreme."

As she rang him up it occurred to him to wonder if he had enough money in his wallet, but when he opened it he saw that his mom had put in a hundred-fifty. He handed her a twenty, then hesitated once he'd gotten his change, trying to remember the rules. "Do I tip you?" he asked.

"Did I do a good job?" she answered.

He gave her a five, which was almost as much as all his stuff had cost, total. Without comment she put it into the community tips jar, then said, "Someone'll bring it out to you. I got to take

13

the next customer."

He planted himself at a wobbly table and wolfed down his food. His elbows on the table kept rocking it back and forth and threatening to knock it over. He couldn't stop looking around the restaurant, and he wished that the whole thing had been leveled, that he'd pulled up and seen the whole neighborhood remodeled. This was the worst, the place being exactly the way he'd remembered it yet leaving him so lonely. The worst were the guys that he recognized but couldn't remember.

He finished his food but there wasn't anyplace for him to go so he just sat there compulsively wiping his mouth with his napkin and looking around nervously, nursing his beer. After forty minutes he started to figure he was going to have to order another one.

There was no line now. Ricky was only sitting about ten feet away from the girl, and he stared at her profile in the sunlight while she stole these few minutes of doing nothing. What did it mean that she pretended not to notice him staring? For she had to be pretending. His beer was finally empty, and he realized that he could use that as an excuse to go and talk to her, so he stood up. She raised her eyebrows as she saw him approach. Ricky decided that he could interpret her expression as wry pleasure.

"You want another?" she asked.

He let a second go by, then said, "What's your name?"

She waited, thinking about it. "Jesse," she said.

"Jesse. Hey, Jesse. I'm Ricky. I used to come here, years ago."

"But then you found something better to do, huh," she said. Something clenched inside him, and he had to remind himself that she didn't mean to be hard—she was only protecting herself, to her he was an unknown quality. And even if he'd been known, well who would be able to blame her even then.

"I don't know if I would say better," he said.

"Well. So how does Vino's compare to the good old days?"

"Exactly the same. Except for the people."

"Were the people much different then? Before you answer, I do got to warn you I like the people now."

"No, no. That's good, you're right to like people."

He said this with such earnestness that she gave him a funny look, before saying, "I've been coming here since I was thirteen and it's basically always been the same people."

Ricky gaped at her. "Thirteen?" he repeated. "How old are you now?"

"Twenty-three."

He kept staring at her a few seconds longer before saying, "I guess that's about right."

"Well. Okay. It *is* right. I was coming here for eight years and everybody knew me, and not even the coolest stoners would sell me a drink. This is where I bought my first legal beer, on my twenty-first birthday. And then I started working here like a week later and have been ever since."

"I must have seen you towards the end. If you really were coming in all the time. Because this was totally my hang-out." He stared at her with great intensity, trying to remember, but then his eyes dulled as the tension drained out. "I guess we wouldn't've paid attention to you, if you were only thirteen."

Jesse raised her eyebrows and made a face like she was about to say something worldly, or witty, or risqué, but when the moment had passed and she hadn't thought of anything she let it go. She did a good job of rearranging her face to look like she was just waiting for Ricky to go on speaking and had been the whole time; he couldn't think of anything any more than she'd been able to, but he did show that he was flustered, and by coming in and saving him she got to retain the upper hand: "So how come you quit coming in for the last, like, ten years?"

Ricky could feel puke-acid fizzing underneath his stomach, and his face starting to burn. He had blown it; he had bored her and she saw him as a baby, and now that that had happened it was fucked, he had fucked up, he was just some dickless piece of shit so he may as well say anything now. Not quite glaring, because he was trying to bear in mind that nothing was this chick's fault, he bit off the words, "I was in prison."

She looked at him differently. The owner walked over

15

and hovered, a gruff older guy that Ricky recognized with that becoming-familiar shock, someone he'd never known by name and who hadn't missed him. And whom he hadn't missed. Jesse grabbed Ricky's pint glass, to make it look like she wasn't just standing at the counter chatting. She refilled the glass, slowly, pouring it without any foam. Before she'd finished the owner had walked away again. Jesse handed Ricky his beer. "I know you didn't technically order that," she said under her breath. "You don't have to pay for it if you don't want to."

"I want to," Ricky said, formal and cold. He took out his wallet and handed Jesse some money.

She took it, rang him up, and made change, without looking at him. As she was putting the money in his hand she asked, "What did you go to jail for?" She sounded subdued, maybe by the seriousness of the subject. "If you don't mind me asking."

Ricky folded the bills and put them in his wallet, put the wallet back in his pocket. The coins he let fall with a clatter into the tips jar. "Wrong place, wrong time," he said. He tried to make light of it as far as possible, although he knew better than to chuckle or anything like that.

She kept looking at him.

He said, "I was driving a car for these guys who were just supposed to pick up some weed. Not even a lot, like a couple pounds. And they wound up shooting the guys we were getting the stuff from."

"Jesus." She was looking at him like he was crazy. "Was it, like, a robbery? A double-cross?"

"No. It was just a fight. One-thing-led-to-another kind of thing. They had some guns, and my friend Tony had a gun, and then they started talking shit."

Jesse kept staring at him. Then she said, "Are you Elly's big brother?"

He stared at her. "You're friends with Elly?"

"No. I don't really know her. But she used to date my boyfriend." She looked down and to the side. "I mean my ex-boyfriend," she said.

3.

He went back to his seat with his refilled beer, and now he sat there twitching and drinking, and fuming. All day, ever since before his release even, he'd felt basically dead. He didn't know how he could feel dead and still suffer but he did. He watched Jesse rub down the counter with a wet washcloth; it was dirty now plus irredeemably stained from all that work it'd done in its time, and Ricky felt like he was drowning in washcloths like that one, like he was at the bottom of a vat of them. Except not at the bottom, because then he would have had the hard floor of the vat underneath him. Like he was in the middle of the vat, a huge vat, all those washcloths soaked in room-temperature water. Everything was eating in on itself, eating in on itself— Ricky couldn't stand it. He forced his hands to relax before they smashed the glass that they held because even if they did smash that glass it wouldn't be like something really *happening*, it would just be more washcloths. He forced his hands to relax but it was hard because it was just so fucking stupid, and it was unbelievable, it was so fucking stupid that it was unbelievable. Did he feel trapped under ice? No—it was a movie set and it was styrofoam ice he was trapped under. If he didn't get out he was going to kill himself, he was going to no shit kill himself, and it wouldn't be like giving up when he did it, either, it really would be the right thing to do.

He was going to do something. He went ahead and drained his beer, slamming it down in three gulps because it would have been pretentious to leave the full glass there, like he'd gotten all carried away. He stood up, marched over to the counter where Jesse was now, tidying, someone else was working the register, that was why he could approach her, why she was relatively accessible. She looked up warily as he approached, he must have looked pretty intense. Without any preamble he said, "You want to go on a date or something?"

She took a step back and laughed, a surprised and not a cruel laugh. "Um. I don't know you," she said.

Sweat was pouring off him. He jammed his hands into his pockets, he figured that if he wiped his face that would only call attention to the sweat. "But I'm not asking you to get married or anything." Sweat dripped into his eye and he yanked a hand out of his pocket to wipe his face off.

"Well, I know you're not asking me to marry you," said Jesse, sounding like whatever bizarre charm his proposal might have had was rapidly wearing off.

He couldn't breathe, colors popped in front of him, he would kick, slam, punch to break down the plaster and to *get the fuck out of this!* "Look, I just got out of prison," he said, raising his voice.

At least her face got a cold-water-splash look at that, which gave him a sort of apocalyptic micro-buzz, but the buzz didn't last. "I know you just got out of prison," she said, numbly.

A big tattooed guy with a beard, a basically friendly-looking guy, came and stood real close to him. "You need to leave, man," he said. "Come on, get out."

It was only out of the corner of his vision that he saw the guy. Keeping his eyes locked on Jesse, he insisted, "You have to help me!"

The big guy put his hand on Ricky's arm: "Man, you got to go."

"No, wait, hold up, it's okay," said Jesse suddenly, "I'll take care of it."

The big guy was devastated, as if he never did stuff like this and now that his help had been rejected he felt like a fool. "Are you *sure*?" he practically wailed.

"Yeah, it's fine," she said, waving him off, coming out from behind the counter and taking Ricky by the arm and heading him toward the front door. "I'll be back in just a second," she said over her shoulder.

On the cracked sidewalk in the press of the hot sunlight she led Ricky a few feet away from the door, to not exactly privacy but its approximation, a gesture offered for lack of the real thing. They stood there with their hands in their pockets, looking at their shoes. Jesse cleared her throat and, not knowing how to start, she asked, "So, like, do you have anybody?"

He thought of Elly, his mom. He said, "I don't know."

She ran her hand through her hair and left it on the top of her head. "It must be really hard," she said, in a giving-everything-its-due tone. "I mean, I can't even imagine. I'd like to help you if you need help, I mean, if I can. But, I mean, when you said 'date,' when you put it like that, it was just kind of weird. Because we don't know each other. But if you need, you know, somebody to talk to, then I'd totally be more than happy to listen."

Ricky started to feel desperate and graspy again. This was just like everything else. When he spoke his tone obviously surprised Jesse: "No, that's not what I meant, I didn't mean something else from what I said. I meant a date, where we kiss at the end."

Jesse stared at him, made an affronted noise, looked off into the distance again. "Um." She shrugged. "I mean, I. Um. I don't know what you expect me to say."

"I don't expect anything. But, I mean, what do you expect *me* to do? Have some line for you?"

"That's how it's usually done, yeah."

"I don't want to bullshit you. I'm just being honest with you here, I just have a feeling about you."

She couldn't look in his face, but she couldn't get away with staring off into the distance anymore either, and her flustered eyes flittered everywhere, as if searching for aid. "I guess if you really feel like you need help, I'm happy to help you," she said helplessly. "But don't call it a date. You can't call it that."

Well, okay, that was fine with Ricky. They could call it

19

whatever she wanted. They could call it hanging out, or having a heart to heart. With a start like this, though, Ricky felt that in the end he'd be able to turn it into something else. "Okay," he said. "Thanks."

Jesse was twisting around on herself. "I need to go back in," she said, turning her body towards the door but unable to be so rude as to just leave with no word from him.

He said, "Can I get your number?"

She recited the number, he repeated it back twice, fixing it in his head. "I need to get back to work," she said.

"Okay," he said. "I'll give you a call. We'll see each other soon."

"All right," she said, and went, not looking back at him, keeping her eyes down. He watched her disappear inside.

And the truth was that, though it really was okay, it wasn't what he'd wanted. He couldn't call it "good." His fantasy had been that she would be charmed by something. Not by him, exactly, but by some quality he'd imagined magically imbuing him. He'd imagined her smiling, things like that, laughing, looking away because he'd made her shy, not upset.

Still, it was something, her distress. It was something, at least.

4.

The next morning the cops came to say Elly was dead. Her apartment had been broken into and she'd been stabbed fourteen times.

His mother was screaming. Ricky sat on the living room couch with his hands hanging between his knees, embarrassed because the two cops were watching. They seemed embarrassed, too. "Why didn't she have time to call 911 while he was busting in the window?" he asked softly, almost to himself. Then he decided that the killer must have broken in before she'd gotten home and had been lying in wait for her. Breaking the window would have made a big noise, but nobody had called the cops, because they were afraid of how stupid they would feel if it turned out they'd called the cops for nothing.

His mother was leaning with her back against the wall opposite him, pushing the heels of her palms against her eyes while she yanked steadily on the hair wrapped up in her fingers. Right now she had her teeth gritted and was making a kind of whining growl. Ricky watched her where she leaned against the fake wood paneling. If his release had been the first time he'd seen her since having gone into jail years ago, if she hadn't come to visit, he wouldn't have recognized her. When he'd gone to jail she'd been at least two hundred and fifty pounds. Now she was a lean little woman, albeit flabby, loose skin and deflated flesh hanging off of her. And then this house. The same one he and Elly had grown up in, but it was practically unrecognizable too. When he and Elly had been kids it'd been a pigsty, not just garbage and old papers and dirty clothes everywhere, carpeting the place, but old food too, slices of pizza moldering for months

21

on paper plates on the scuffed-up coffee table, fries forgotten in their McDonald's bags that had gone translucent from the grease. Now the place was spic and span. The house he and Elly had grown up in.

His mother stalked over to him without seeming to use her eyes, bent over at the waist, pressed her hot wet angry face against his, grabbed him around the neck with her arms and tugged him towards her. "Christ!" she roared. When the call had come he'd seen that she'd had no feeling of surprise to distract her from the pain. It was the kind of thing you were always secretly convinced would happen.

He hugged her back. His big arms were awkward around her frail waist and up her back. "I'm sorry, Mom," he said.

After half a minute or so she detached herself and walked towards another wall. Then she stood facing it, one hand on her hip, the other pinching the bridge of her nose. Her back was to Ricky. "Fuck," she said.

Ricky sat there. Then he went to the bathroom, switched on the hard fluorescent light and also the ventilator fan, to cover any noise. He locked the door behind him, went over to the toilet, and knelt before it, lifting its lid. Then he stuck three fingers into the back of his throat and kept jabbing them back there until he finally puked. Luckily he'd eaten a lot the night before, plus had had a big breakfast before the cops had come, so the puke came out in a torrent, crumpled his stomach and twisted it around. When it was over, it left him gasping raggedly into the bowl, his hot face cold and bathed with sweat, his hands shaking, eyes watery, mouth scraped and sour, lips coated with slime, his whole self blasted. He stayed there a long time, but eventually he felt obligated to go be with his mother.

The cops were still there when he got out of the bathroom. Heavyset guys. They asked about the victim, were interested when it turned out Ricky had seen her the day before, asked him about that. But for the most part their questions were about Elly's general habits and it was his mom who fielded them. After a while she excused herself to go to the bathroom. Alone with the cops, Ricky, who was sitting with his elbows on his parted knees and his hands clasping each other, said, "Am I a suspect?"

Both the cops looked at him in surprise. "Why do you ask that?" asked the heavier one.

Ricky said, "I'm on parole."

"You're on parole? What're you on parole for?"

"Driving a car for some other guys who wound up killing some people."

That obviously interested them both, but they didn't say anything for a little bit. Then the less fat one said, "Is that so." Ricky's mom came back and the cops didn't pursue the subject, probably out of decency. They must have figured Ricky wasn't going anywhere. And then, maybe they really honestly felt like he hadn't killed his sister. Ricky was miffed that they hadn't known he was on parole. It seemed like a real lapse.

The family—which was just Aunt Lenora, who'd stayed fat, and her two soft teenagers—showed up, and the cops left not long after. Aunt Lenora was crying, not less hard than Ricky's mom, exactly, but with less anger, with more stunned shock in her bereavement. She hugged Ricky and gave him a wet kiss on the cheek, pressing her moist face to his, then planted herself at the kitchen table and cried along with Ricky's mom, one arm around her sister's shoulders and the other hand gripping her sister's near arm, their foreheads touching as they wept. "Oh, Shoshona!" said Lenora.

Ricky stood in the kitchen for a few minutes, respectfully trying to not stare at his mom and aunt but at the same time trying not to seem like he was ignoring them. Finally he couldn't stand feeling stupid anymore what with the way he was just standing there, so he went back to the living room without the women seeming to notice. He sat on the couch and stared back at his chubby cousins, who were staring at him in terror. Finally he couldn't stand that anymore either, so he got up and went back to the kitchen. There he stood in the doorway for a while, waiting to be acknowledged, until, when he wasn't, he said, "Mom," and, again, "Mom." The second time she and Aunt

Lenora both looked up at him.

Face burning, he said, "Mom, I've got to go. I've just got to get out of here."

He'd been steeling himself for her to feel betrayed and shocked, but her face opened generously to him and she shook her head, saying, "Oh, of course, baby, of course," releasing him. Her generosity was so unexpected that he didn't know what to do at first; then he turned and walked out, not saying goodbye to Aunt Lenora or her kids. Outside he unlocked his mom's car, slid into the driver's seat, turned on the ignition, and pulled out into the street, managing to keep his movements precise and keep himself from trembling.

He left the thin blue crumbling ribbon of his mom's road and got to Baseline, went down Baseline a mile or so, then pulled into another side street and a couple streets later started going around a randomly chosen block. Where could he go? He couldn't go see Elly. There weren't any friends. There was a middle-aged black guy in a wifebeater standing in front of his house looking at his scruffy lawn, and the fifth time Ricky drove past the guy flipped him off. Ricky went back to Baseline, deciding to go back onto the freeway and across town to Vino's.

5.

As Ricky pulled into the terrible Vino's parking lot he was scanning it, as if these were the old days and he might recognize someone's car, so he wasn't paying attention to the potholes and he smacked the car right into one. It bounced and as it came down the pavement hit the undercarriage, and Ricky heard and felt the jagged concrete scrape along the bottom. He thought he might have really damaged the vehicle and, shaking, he got out. He double- and triple-checked the car, but still couldn't get his breathing under control.

Jesse wasn't inside Vino's. Behind the counter there was some guy. He thought about telling this dude that his sister Elly had been killed, but that was stupid. Besides, Elly had hung out here, and for all he knew she'd been friends with this guy. What if he went to this stranger for comfort and he turned out to be more upset than Ricky? He ordered one of those fancy microbrewery beers, then stood there at the counter holding the pint glass. Then he pulled himself together and walked away from the counter, pretending like he was supposed to meet someone, some friend, that he didn't see yet.

There was another room off the main dining room, and Ricky headed there. Lots of tables but few people; also an unmanned, unstocked bar. Ricky was horrified to find that there was a guy sitting at that bar sobbing, leaning his forehead into the palm of his hand, tears and snot on his red face. On the other side of the room were some people sitting and eating at a table, trying to ignore the crying guy. Vino's had the music turned up loud, that was why Ricky hadn't heard the weeping from out in the front room. He was already walking in now and

25

it would have been weird to turn around and head back.

He sat at a table that was equally far from the crying guy and from the group of friends. At first he tried not to look at the crying guy, but the guy seemed oblivious to his surroundings, so Ricky decided it couldn't hurt to check him out more openly. He was thin and little, in a punk-band T-shirt, with red hair and a reddish complexion made even more so by the blood rushing into his face—his nose was kind of a beak. He wasn't even trying to choke back his sobs and cry quietly. Watching him, Ricky had the familiar feeling that reality was on the other side from him of a soundproofed, unbreakable, plexiglass wall, a dirty wall that you couldn't see through clearly. Then something occurred to him and, excited, he stood up and carried his beer over to the guy. The guy seemed not to even notice him coming. Ricky stood beside him and gingerly touched him on the shoulder, and said, "Hey, man. Is your name Paul?"

The guy sniffed a bunch of snot back into his throat and blinked and looked up at Ricky. "Yeah?" he said.

"Dude," said Ricky. "I'm Ricky. I'm Elly's big brother."

Paul broke out in a fresh flurry of crying and embraced Ricky, who patted him on the back and said, "It's going to be all right, man. It's going to be all right."

"It's not. She's dead." That was true, so Ricky didn't say anything back.

It was like Ricky had broken the spell or something; Paul got himself under control. Wiping his eyes and nose on his skinny forearm, he sniffed again and said, "Elly told me you were going to be getting out of prison soon."

"Yesterday."

Paul stared at him, stricken. "Did you even get to see her?"

"Yeah. Yesterday."

"And then as soon as you get out someone . . . as soon as you get out, this happens? You must be . . . Jesus, man. . . ." And Paul leaned in to give him another hug, which Ricky accepted. "You must be so fucked up over this," Paul said, and cried a little to punctuate it.

Ricky held him, uncomfortably. He said, "Do you think it was that guy she was dating?"

Paul squeezed him and shook his head. Because Paul had his head buried in between Ricky's neck and shoulder, when he shook it he rocked Ricky's own head back and forth. "I don't know," he said. "Maybe, but how do I know?"

"That guy Ted. Elly said he was a thug. Why did she call him a thug?"

"Well, because he was. But I don't know if that means he killed her." When Ricky didn't say anything, Paul let go of him, leaned back and looked at him. It seemed like he was waking up from something as he studied Ricky, and said, "But hey, man. They'll find whoever it is."

"Sure."

"We can't worry about that shit, man. They're going to get him. If it even is a him. The cops'll do that."

"No, yeah, I know."

Ricky was facing the doorway to the front room and Paul had his back to it, so Ricky was the one who saw Jesse hurry in, her keys dangling from her hand. She stopped short when she saw Ricky looking at her, then looked even more freaked out when she saw who he was holding. "Hey, guys," she said.

"Oh, sweetie," said Paul, and got off his stool and hugged her tenderly and kissed her on the cheek. Jesse squirmed and pointedly did not look at Ricky. "Okay," she said. "Hey, Paul." At that he seemed to feel that something was inappropriate and he let her go. Jesse went on: "I didn't know you guys knew each other." There was something accusatory in her voice, or defensive.

"We don't," said Ricky. "I just. . . ." He stopped, not sure how he should explain.

Paul said, "Honey, Ricky here is Elly's big brother."

"I know," said Jesse, and then, under her breath (even though Ricky was right there and could hear her just as well as Paul could), she said, "Don't call me 'honey' anymore, Paul."

Paul just looked at her. You would have thought that he

27

hadn't heard her reprimand, except for the way his whole self *stopped* for a moment, like he was recalibrating. He said, "Ricky just walked up to me and introduced himself."

Jesse looked from one to the other of them. "How did he know who you were?"

"I don't know, it was weird. I guess he just had a feeling."

Ricky was trying to figure out a tactful way to explain how he'd guessed, but Jesse was too exasperated to leave him a chance. "Okay," she said. "Well, that's amazing, I guess."

"Are you working today, honey?" said Paul. "I didn't think you worked today."

This time she didn't tell him not to call her "honey," like she couldn't be expected to ask him to stop every single time he did it. "No," she said. "They called me and asked me to come and, you know. . . ." She trailed off, probably not wanting to explain in front of Ricky that she'd been called because Paul was making a scene. Impatiently, she said, "How are you getting home? Do you need somebody to take you home?"

"I don't know."

"Well do you have your car here?"

"No, it's broken, I got someone to drop me off."

"Well then you need a ride home."

"Okay, except it's not much of a walk," said Paul, and he started to cry again, but just a little this time. "I just had to get out of the apartment. When I heard."

"I know," Jesse said, wearily, and guiltily, because it was wrong to be sharp with him when he was suffering. She took Paul under her arm. As she was hugging Paul, her concerned eyes went to Ricky. "And what about you?" she asked. "Jesus, I'm sorry. How are *you* doing?"

Ricky was looking at Paul's back with distaste. Now he locked his eyes on Jesse's glistening ones, and said, "I'm dealing with it."

"You just, you know. Got home, and stuff. I mean, did you even get to see her, at least?"

"I did. I did get to see her." Then he said, "Hey, are we still

28

on to go out?"

Jesse's eyes got wide and panicked, and Paul straightened up and looked at them both, frowning curiously. Jesse said, "Uh, sure. Let's talk about it later, though, okay?"

"Sure. I'll call you in a little while. I still have your number." And he repeated it back to her, to show that he'd remembered.

She looked like she might have preferred that he hadn't done that, but all she said was, "Okay. Give me a call. And especially let me know if you need anything, what with, you know."

"Okay."

Paul was still looking back and forth at them, confused and interested. "Wait, hold up," he said, "so *you* guys know each other? How do *you* know each other?"

"We met yesterday," said Jesse helplessly. "Here. When he came to get a beer."

"Yeah," said Ricky. "It was just like with you and me, man. These things happen."

At home, in the dark, his mother's sobs morphed into snores. There was pain but underneath it reality was undented.

Ricky had a weird dream with Paul in it. He didn't remember it after he woke up, except they say part of you always remembers your dreams.

There were two dreams overlaid on top of each other, woven together. The first was a standard Ricky-dream: he was being chased by something through a dark labyrinth. Whatever was chasing Ricky was inexorable and gaining on him, so that Ricky wished it would go ahead and catch him, so Ricky could quit running.

In the other dream he was fucking. He realized he was buttfucking Paul and it freaked him out. It felt weird, Paul's asshole had too tight a grip on Ricky's dick; Ricky worried that he might be hurting himself. Sometimes he could convince himself that he wasn't really buttfucking Paul, and then he was able to see a girl there instead, on her back. Her big titties bounced and under her curly black hair her face was a blur. That was nicer than buttfucking Paul, but there was still a menace hidden under the secret of that blur. But then the girl's titties wouldn't be as big anymore, they'd be regular-sized like Elly's; and then it would be Elly's face, not the blur anymore, it would be Elly he was fucking. That felt good, but it was horrible that it felt good, and he'd push the vision away, and again it'd be Paul he was buttfucking. Then he'd push that away, and it would again be Elly, or the big-titty girl. The principle within himself that conjured their ghostly flesh kaleidoscoped continually through all three, the dream-bodies squirming and roiling beneath him.

He scared himself awake and lay in the darkness to which his eyes had not adapted, listening to the creaking and clicking of the always-settling house. Listening for his mother, but there was no sound of her anymore. Elly was dead. At the thought, it was like his abdominal cavity was washed in fart-smelling acid, like his brain swelled to where it was going to pop through his forehead. He tried to remember the dream, whatever it had been. But it was all gone. He never remembered it in his whole life.

6.

The next day the cops came again. It was early enough that it wouldn't interfere with Ricky's date, and he was glad, because he wanted to help, be a part of things.

He planted himself on the scratchy sofa, beside his mom. She absently patted his knee. Aunt Lenora was still there, she was spending a couple nights at the house. The two cops were sitting on the loveseat catty-cornered to the sofa—not the same cops as yesterday, these guys were in suits, though they were still big fat guys. They apologized about bugging Ricky and his mom in this difficult time. His mom let them finish, then said, "It was that piece of shit Ted, wasn't it?"

The cops said that was what they were trying to find out.

"She was scared of him. She told me a hundred times that this was going to happen."

"But she still stuck with this Ted guy anyway?"

"She has bad taste in men. She takes after her mom that way." She started to cry and they all waited respectfully for her to finish. Ricky felt like he should be putting his arm around her or something, but he wasn't sure of himself and didn't want to screw up in front of the cops. He couldn't help but give her an embarrassed glance. Yesterday she'd seemed noble in her epic grief, but today he felt guiltily ashamed of her, like she was the same old mom after all, like he'd stupidly been taken in by a ratty old Santa costume.

His mom finished crying. She gave a couple last sniffles, like punctuation marks, and said, "Okay."

The cops asked for pictures of Ted, and of Elly with Ted. Shoshona fetched four huge photo albums for them. "The

31

photos are all mixed in," she said. "I don't really do them chronologically."

The cops opened the top album to the first page. "Who's this?" one asked.

"That's Elly when she was a teenager. And Ricky."

"And who's that with them?" He looked at Lenora; "Oh, sorry, it's you."

"No," said Shoshona, "that was me."

"Wow. You lost some weight."

Lenora laughed with nervous offendedness. Shoshona said, "Yeah, I guess I did."

Both of the fat cops were staring fascinatedly at the photo of the former Shoshona. "How'd you do it?" asked the second one. "Weight Watchers? Stomach staples?"

"Yeah, what's your secret?"

"Oh, a lot of things changed around here after Ricky got sent away."

Now the cops raised their heads with new interest, looking from Ricky to his mom and back. "Oh, yeah?" said the first one. "Tell us about that." Meaning her weight loss, not Ricky getting sent away.

She told them about how the place had been a wreck the whole time the kids were growing up; how she'd been a fat slob. There'd been food, garbage, and dirty ancient laundry everywhere—and maybe that had been partly to blame for the wrong turns Ricky had made. (Ricky put his hand on her forearm and murmured that that wasn't true, but his mom kept going like she hadn't noticed.) Then when Ricky went to jail, everything changed. The very morning after his sentencing she'd woken up early, done some cleaning for the first time in years, and had walked around the block, though she hadn't made it halfway before she'd had to sit gasping on the curb. But she'd kept at it every day until she'd been strong enough to join a gym and also do aerobics at home. Meanwhile, she'd cleaned up the house, throwing away almost everything. There had been a few months when most of her and Elly's furniture had consisted of folding chairs and card tables, until she'd saved up some money at the new job she'd gotten as a cashier at Home Depot, where she was now a manager.

The second cop whistled, and the first one said, "Pretty impressive."

"I guess I just got inspired once my boy got taken away."

Ricky smiled tightly at his mother, proud of her but not wanting to look like he was taking credit for anything. All those childhood memories of her glaring for hours at the TV, only rousing herself to occasionally bark at him and Elly, they all seemed so far removed from reality that their vividness only made them more surreal.

They got back on track. The cop wanted to hear more about Ted, and Shoshona told the tales in a professional tone. Ted had hit Elly a few times, once bad enough to leave marks on her face so that she'd called in sick till they'd mostly faded.

Ricky was shocked. "She never told me that."

Ted had been known to stick a knife to her neck and threaten to slit her throat. Ricky had known that Elly'd called him "the thug," but all this was news. Shoshona finished by saying, "Why on earth don't you go and arrest him?"

The cops didn't look at each other. "Well," said the first one, "the truth is we're not sure where he is."

For a few seconds Shoshona said nothing, then: "Well, that proves he did it, right?"

"Not necessarily."

"What in the world else could it mean?"

"Not at liberty to speculate about that right now."

"Yeah, well, you have to say that shit."

"We're interested in talking to him," said the second cop. "Any idea where we might be able to find him?"

Shoshona drew her head back, a gesture with sort of an ironic threat. "Now why the hell would you ask me that?"

"We have to ask this stuff, ma'am."

"That fucker stabbed my little baby, in the face. You think I'm hiding him?"

"Nobody's suggesting that."

"Because let me tell you what, if I did know where that little piece of shit was, there wouldn't be nothing but a stain left of him. . . ."

Ricky cut in with, "Hey, don't say that, Mom," because it had occurred to him that having Ted pop up with his brains blown out might be doable, and if that happened he didn't want his mom on record as having said she'd kill him.

But she stared at him aghast. "Do you think I give a fuck?" she demanded. "Do you honestly think that I give a fuck?" Ricky froze, with no idea how to answer.

Shoshona turned back to the cops. "All I know about Ted is that he's a piece of shit and that's it. I wish I knew more. I told her I didn't want to hear it, and that was the biggest mistake of my life, I guess. After he beat up her face I told her I didn't want to hear any more about that son of a bitch, unless it was 'Mom, I'm leaving him.' I thought I was being tough. But instead, maybe if she'd been able to tell me about what was going on, I could've, I don't know, I could've. . . ."

Shoshona started crying. All the men squirmed and tried not to look at her; Lenora rubbed her back.

She stopped crying again pretty quick. The first cop said, "I know you're upset, and I wish I could leave you alone right now, but we have to keep asking you stuff." Shoshona shrugged. The cop went on: "If Ted was so abusive, how come Elly stayed with him?"

Shoshona stared at him, her head tilted to the side, like she really didn't understand the question: "What? But I already told you—she wasn't good with men." Then she started to sob harder than before.

The cops waited in embarrassment. Lenora put her arm around Shoshona again and this time drew her all the way down and into her bulk, laying her heavy arm around her shoulder. Ricky reached out and touched his mother on the side, and felt her flinch away from him. Probably he'd startled her. He waited for her to apologize to him, so he could assure her that it was no big deal, but the seconds passed and she made no move to do so, she just lay there with her flesh clenched away from him.

They sat there waiting. It was unbearable. And Ricky figured that he was useless anyway, because there was nothing he was likely to know about Ted, because he'd been in jail for years. Elly hadn't even written much about him in her letters—not like with Paul. If it had been Paul, he could have told them stuff. Ricky'd seen a photo of the guy the other day at her apartment, but that was it. Elly hadn't even told him that Ted beat her up.

Reality had gotten dense, time and space had transformed from an ether into something like a clear molasses. You could see through it, from one point to another, but its consistency was too thick and viscous for the magic spirit of life to move freely between those points. Instead, it went like air wheezing through a throat in which food was lodged. Ricky was choking with his whole being. They were all here in this room together, and these moments and seconds and minutes were all collected in the one place, but the clear gunk held them suspended. Ricky stood up and marched into the kitchen as if he were going to get himself a glass of water.

He stood in there for a little bit. He already had his keys in his pocket, and he calculated his trajectory from here to the front door. He would have to go through the living room where everyone was gathered, but he figured he could get through there and out to the car in the front yard before they stopped him. He wasn't doing any good here. Plus he had that date with Jesse that he needed to get to.

He made a break for it, walking first through the living room and looking at its occupants only out the corners of his eyes. He made it through the front door and didn't bother locking it behind him, and got into the car and pulled out of the driveway. As soon as he was on the road his breath came easier. It was still too early to go meet Jesse, but he could drive around some.

Maybe it hadn't been smart to make it look like he was running out—he was on parole for a murder case, after all—it wouldn't be hard to provoke the cops into poking around about him. But he was safe in the knowledge that he'd had nothing to do with Elly getting killed. So let them ask whatever they wanted. It wouldn't hurt him to be involved in the investigation. That would be just fine.

7.

He'd forgotten the cell phone his mom had given him, so Ricky had to find a payphone to call Jesse on—before he'd gone to jail there had been three times as many around, seemed like. Finally he found one in an Exxon parking lot. Jesse told him her address. Ricky didn't recognize the street name and he kept screwing up the directions when repeating them back. He remembered how easily he'd memorized her phone number, and decided he was good with numbers but bad with directions.

He managed to make his way to her house. It was weird, this homecoming, the way bursts of recognition alternated with revelations of cavernous mystery around the ordinary corners.

She lived in a very big house with a tiny scabby front yard of dirt and weeds. From the four cars in the front yard he could tell that she had roommates. The once-white paint on the house's weathered boards was chipped and in places completely worn away, in a way that it might not have been if the same people who'd lived there had also owned the place.

Ricky went to the front door and rang the doorbell. Nobody came at first, but he knew people were home because he could hear the TV inside.

Finally Jesse opened the door, looking frazzled. "Um. Hey," she said. "I have to finish just a couple things before I go. You can come inside, or. . . ." She trailed off, and there was a pause during which it felt like she'd prefer him to wait outside. She wound up saying, "Come on in," though.

Ricky went inside. One of Jesse's roommates was sitting in front of the TV smoking a cigarette, ashing into a hubcap already overflowing with butts and cinders. Another was snoring in his bedroom, a chubby guy in his boxers and a too-tight T-shirt—he had left his door halfway open. Jesse bustled around. She'd cooked lunch for everyone, though she assured Ricky that she hadn't eaten any herself, so as to stay hungry for him; she'd meant to have the dishes done before Ricky arrived, but she'd gotten caught up in other chores. Ricky stood in the living room and waited for her to finish.

It was weird, just standing there without saying anything to the roommate who was sitting right there, staring at the television. To make conversation, Ricky asked if he could bum a cigarette.

The roommate considered a long time, then said, "Nah, man. They're expensive, and everyone's always bumming them."

Ricky blushed, but stayed cheerful as he said, "That's cool. I shouldn't have one, anyway. I actually quit years ago, back when I was in prison."

The roommate made a face. "You were in prison?"

"Oh, yeah, you know." Then Ricky waited for the roommate to ask him how long, for what, stuff like that, but he didn't.

Jesse finished doing the dishes and they left and got in the car. Ricky started to drive off, then saw that she was still putting on her seatbelt. He slammed on the brakes to give her a chance to buckle up before they got started, nearly sending her right into the windshield. She got her seatbelt on. Ricky was glad that he'd also remembered to wear his.

He backtracked through the unfamiliar, ordinary neighborhood the way he'd come, heading for someplace where he could regain his bearings. "So," he said. "How was your day so far?"

Jesse shrugged. "Oh, it's good." Then, after a moment, she said, "Uh. It's been pretty stressful, actually. What with everything. Earlier I went over to take care of Paul."

"Is he okay?"

"Oh, you know. He's pretty upset. . . . I mean, I'm sorry, I know you're, you know, even more upset. . . ."

"You guys dated after he and Elly broke up?"

"Yeah, for like six months. We just broke up."

"But y'all're still good friends, I guess."

"Not really," said Jesse, and laughed. "I mean, I don't hate him or anything. But I guess hanging out with him every day would probably not be my first choice, no. But what with what happened. . . . Elly really meant a lot to him."

"He seems like a good guy, I guess. I know he wasn't always the best guy for Elly, but. . . ." He let the thought trail off.

Jesse nodded. "It's not like it matters now." She looked quickly at Ricky and said, "Sorry."

"It's okay," he said. Jesse nodded again and turned to look out her window. It seemed to Ricky that the thoughts and remarks were passing between them with remarkable ease, considering the circumstances.

She asked where they were going and he told her Ruby Tuesday. It was the closest thing to a nice restaurant that he could remember the directions to. He'd been strongly tempted to take her to a movie—a pretty conventional datey thing to do, he thought, enough so that no one could find fault with it, and it would be such a relief, a balm, to be able to sit in the dark and know that she was with him, had chosen to be so, and yet that he didn't have to think of things to say. But his gut warned him that a movie wouldn't be right. He did want to duck the strain of having to put things into words, but in a movie theater there would be the even greater strain of an unaccomplished duty hanging over him, all the words he was supposed to be thinking of and saying but had proved too dumb and too pussy to be able to, all the words and gestures and almost invisible movements of soul that he was supposed to be drawing out from Jesse and absorbing and trying to understand, all those dangerous but necessary opportunities.

So after he'd grabbed his space in the parking deck of the Park Plaza Mall, he led Jesse to Ruby Tuesday instead of the multiplex. He debated for a sweaty moment on whether or not to try to hold her hand, then decided to hold off for now.

At Ruby Tuesday they ordered the salad bar and went to fill

their plates while the waitress was getting their drinks. It was weird being at the salad bar together, in front of all the other people grazing. What were they supposed to talk about? His dead sister? Paul? They stuck to attempted witticisms about the food.

At the table Jesse munched on the taco salad she'd fixed herself and said, "Thanks, this is good."

The fact that she'd thanked him meant that he was paying, so Ricky figured this was definitely a date. "Yeah, it is," he said. "I can't get used to how good food is in restaurants. Like that pizza the other day at Vino's. . . . Anyway, all I'm saying is that this sure is a lot better than what we got in jail." Then he felt dumb because, duh, of course it was better than what he'd had in jail.

But Jesse wasn't looking at him like he was dumb. Head bent over her plate as she shoveled food into her mouth, her eyes stayed fixed on his face, and she asked, "Was it as awful there as it seems like it would be?"

"I guess so. Probably."

"What was the worst thing that happened to you?"

Ricky dropped his eyes, pushed himself back in his seat, and shook his head. "No. I don't want to talk about that."

"Oh Jesus. I'm sorry. I'm such an asshole."

"No, it's cool, *I'm* sorry, for being weird about it."

"Oh my God, are you kidding? It was an idiot question to ask you."

"No. It makes total sense that you would want to ask. I just, you know. . . ."

"Okay. Well. Anyway. Let's change the subject away from my bonehead goof."

"Okay." He might even have gone ahead and told her about the worst thing that had happened to him in prison, except that the worst thing hadn't actually happened, so it would have been hard to explain. "It wasn't all bad."

"Really?"

"Yeah. The guards would let us all out of our cells all at

40

once, one day a week. Aryan Brotherhood, the Crips, the Bloods, the whole gang. And all those hundreds of us would do a big musical number, like from *Jailhouse Rock*. The guards would play the instruments."

"Really?"

"No. I'm kidding."

Jesse laughed hard enough to spit out her Coke. Ricky was expecting a quick, polite chuckle, but she kept laughing, her eyes squeezed together above her big chipmunk cheeks, yet still locked on his with honest, whole delight. Finally Ricky accepted that her reaction did indeed seem genuine, and let his own mouth spread in pleasure.

Still grinning, Jesse wiped up the Coke that she'd spat onto the table. "So, okay," she said, "jail totally sucks. Duly noted."

"Actually, there were . . . I mean, it did suck. But there were some good effects."

"Like?"

"Like Elly. Before I went away, she and I . . . well, I wasn't a very good big brother. I saw her a lot. Maybe more than most big brothers see their little sisters, even. And it was . . . well. Anyway, when I went away, I was afraid we would, you know, whatever. But while I was in jail, we stayed close."

"How'd y'all manage that? Did she come visit all the time?"

"No. I mean, she came to visit. But not super-often. I wasn't crazy about having her come into that place. Or having her see me, you know, like that. But the main way wasn't seeing her in person at all, it was mainly from reading her letters."

"Oh, yeah? She wrote you a lot of letters?"

"Yeah. She wrote me every few days. But it wasn't just the amount. It was, I don't know. They were, uh, special."

"That's really nice, that she was a good letter-writer. It's, like, a vanishing thing." Jesse took another sip of her Coke and moved food around her plate with the fork, then said, "So tell me about her letters." Then, hastily, she added, "If you want to, I mean."

"Sure. It was, um. I don't really know how to explain them.

41

They were really chatty and jokey, she was funny. I hadn't known how funny she was. Like, that she was funny enough to be able to show off about it. And she would tell stories. About her life, her friends, then later on her boyfriends. Like Paul. I read so much about Paul for years, this whole big saga about their relationship, that I felt like I knew him. I wanted to get the next letter and find out what was going to happen next with Paul. It was, I don't know, just ordinary stuff she told me about, ordinary high-school girl stuff, and then ordinary college-girl stuff. At least, I guess it was ordinary college stuff, I wouldn't really know. And then about that job she had, and the people there and the stuff she did."

"Did you write letters back to her?"

"No. Or, I mean, yeah. But just stuff like, How are you, Thank you for your letters, Everything here is fine, Sincerely, Ricky. It wasn't like the way she did it. She created this whole world. Not out of the things that happened, they were all pretty boring, if you thought about them. But out of the voice she wrote with. The things she saw about people and the way she put stuff together. She made it so that it meant something. And I just, I liked that world better than the one I was in. I wanted to be in hers. It was just sort of like, there was something about it that meant something."

Jesse looked at him, absently stirring her salad. "Yeah, I bet. Especially considering, I mean, the world you were in must have sucked, to put it mildly."

"Yeah. But, plus, isn't that what everybody wants when they start trying to hook up with a new person? Is to be taken out of the world they're in? Like, it isn't so much that the one we're already in is awful, even though usually it is. It's just more like you want the other person to help you break *out*. You want more space."

Jesse was looking at him more intently now, had started excitedly and compulsively sticking food in her mouth. "Yeah," she said. "Yeah, you get to feeling so cooped up. Like you're going to go crazy. Or, no, I guess it would be a relief to go crazy.

42

Everything seems so fake and pointless."

"Yeah. Yeah."

They ate in silence a while. Then Jesse said, shyly, "Maybe it's stupid, but it almost seems like there would be almost good things about being in jail. Like, not *good*, I don't mean, but . . . maybe things would at least be clearer. Like, you wouldn't have all these weird obligations that appear out of nowhere. You'd have to stay alive and try to keep from getting your ass kicked and that'd be it. There wouldn't be any confusion." Seeming to suddenly hear herself, she laughed in horror and said, "Oh my God, what a stupid bitch I sound like! I'm sorry."

Ricky sat there holding his fork over his plate, looking at the table, not sure how to reply. "Prison really sucked," he said finally.

Jesse sobered. "Yeah," she said. "Yeah. Of course it did. I'm sorry."

"No, don't be sorry."

"No, I am. It was a dumb thing to say. I was letting my, I don't know, daydreams get away with me, or something."

"I didn't mean anything. I just meant—you know—that it was bad."

Jesse gazed at him a moment longer. Then, as if she were making a decision, or signing something, she reached across the table and put her hand on top of his where it lay on the table. He rotated it so that their palms touched, then closed his fingers over hers.

8.

They talked about regular stuff a while. Like, they talked about their families. Ricky told her about his mom's transformation. Jesse talked about her mom and dad, whom she'd gone to church with this past weekend. She claimed she'd outgrown their whole religion thing long ago, but still participated in it with them because she felt guilty. Towards the end of their date, Ricky asked Jesse if she knew Ted.

She made a face. "Yeah, I know him. We went to high school together." It had already come up that Jesse'd gone to high school at Parkview—Ricky and Elly had gone to Little Rock High, and Elly and Jesse had never met each other. Which was weird, because as Jesse and Ricky talked about Elly it became clear that, even in spite of having gone to different schools, the girls' worlds had intersected everywhere. In terms of guys, at least.

"The cops think he killed Elly."

Jesse made another face, one that was harder to interpret. "I heard that," she said. "Are they sure?" Maybe the face meant that she had once had to be kind to Ted, the way she'd had to be kind to Paul yesterday and earlier today, the way she was being kind to Ricky now, and that she couldn't entirely reverse gears, not all at once.

Ricky said, "No, they're not sure. Not officially anyway. But they're looking for him and can't find him. And Elly said he was a thug. That was one of the last things she ever said to me. What about you? What do you think?"

Jesse paused. He could see her really, actually going over it in her mind. Then she nodded and said, "Yeah, he probably did it." They were both quiet a second, then she added, "Isn't that always the first suspect anyway? The boyfriend?"

"Especially when the boyfriend beats her up and bruises her face."

"Did he do that? I didn't know."

"Yeah. Is that a surprise? Like, to you, to someone who knows him?"

She shrugged. "No."

They changed the subject to something more date-appropriate, but before long it drifted back to Ted again. "I don't guess you have any idea where he could be?" asked Ricky.

She looked at him like he was crazy. "Of course not," she said.

"No, I don't mean like that, like you're keeping a secret. I just meant, like, maybe you might know places he hangs out, stuff like that. Stuff the cops wouldn't necessarily know."

"I don't know any more than anyone else. And I think he just went to all the usual places. Except I think I remember that he used to hang out at that skeezy Joe Bear's place. I guess maybe he still does. Except, I mean, if he knows the cops are looking for him then maybe he's not hanging out anywhere."

"Where did you say? Some kind of Bears place?"

"It's French," she said, and spelled it for him: Jaubert's. "It's this creepy place out by Kanis Park, on Asher. I've never been in there."

"Did he go there really often?"

"Oh, I don't know. Probably not as often as he hung out at Vino's and Juanita's and all the regular places. I just always remember it because he's the only one I ever heard of going there."

"Why's it creepy?"

"Because it just looks like it is. Like the kind of place where there are fights. Also Paul told me that he would drag Elly there and the whole vibe really freaked her out."

Ricky thought it over. "You think they might have any idea where Ted might be?"

"The people who hang out at Jaubert's? I don't know why they would."

"Might be a good place to start, though. For someone that was trying to find the guy."

"I guess. Mention it to the cops, maybe."

He drove her home, getting more and more agitated over whether or not he should kiss her and, if so, how he should choreograph it. It turned out to be a moot point, since she hopped out of the car as soon as he pulled up to her front yard, though she did stand just outside the car and wave at him. "Okay, thanks," she said, "I had a nice time. Thanks for buying me lunch."

Ricky set off towards Kanis Park. He turned the radio on, to kill the quiet. Then he spent the rest of the drive flipping through the stations. Sometimes there'd be something decent playing, good enough for him to sing along in snatches, but he always compulsively switched to see what was playing elsewhere.

The worst thing that had ever happened to him in jail, which hadn't actually happened (or, he supposed, the worst thing that had ever almost happened to him): there'd been this one guy, Larry, this super-effeminate older guy who'd been in for five years and who most everybody fucked with. He was always nice to Ricky, and Ricky was nice to him. In the yard one day Bernard, this meaty smooth-scalped redneck with swastika tattoos, had been taunting Larry for the benefit of his jeering posse, describing all the shit he was going to do to him while Larry trembled and, trying to smile ingratiatingly, kept repeating, "Okay, well, you're in charge, so, you know, if you decide to do that, if you decide to do that, Bernard, there's no way I can stop you."

Ricky stood there, almost but not quite in the small circle of onlookers. He knew he ought to do something, but couldn't visualize the action he was supposed to be bringing into existence. The chance to fulfill some requirement was definitely slipping away, though. He forced himself to say something, but all that came out was "Hey."

He'd said it in a calm tone, at a casual, conversational volume. But Bernard reacted like Ricky had shouted. He snapped around, glared at Ricky with excited outrage. "You sticking up for this faggot?" he said.

Ricky blinked. He felt scared, but it was more like stage fright than fear of physical danger. "I, just, you know," he said.

"What did you say?! I know what?!"

"Just, you know."

"Do *you* want to know something? I'm going to fuck you, you faggot." Cheers from Bernard's friends. "Me and my boys are going to hold you down in the showers and take turns ripping your asshole out."

Bernard waited. Ricky just kind of looked at him in the middle of all those guys, hooting and hollering.

"Well?" said Bernard finally. "You got something to say about that, faggot?"

Ricky opened his mouth and shut it. He shrugged, self-conscious.

Bernard didn't even bother to make fun of him not being able to talk. He just pointed at him and said, "I'm going to rape you, faggot." Then it was time to go in, and the laughing crowd dispersed.

After that, in the showers, Ricky would clench himself even more tightly than before. And when Bernard and his friends were in there with him, he felt so freaked out that it was like it was already happening. Bernard and his skinhead buddies would murmur and whisper to each other, and then burst out laughing. There was no proof they were talking about Ricky—even the malicious edge in their voices didn't necessarily mean much—but it fucked with the rhythm of Ricky's heartbeat even so.

But the thing was that nothing ever happened. Ricky spent hundreds of hours wondering how he would react, figuring out what he would do to resist and how he would live with himself after that resistance inevitably failed. But all that work of psyching himself up proved to be for nothing. Even after

Bernard got paroled, Ricky assumed that he had deputized some of his cronies to someday fuck Ricky up, and he stayed ready for something to happen. But nothing ever did. Not that he was complaining. Obviously, he was relieved that the threat had never come true, and that he hadn't had to deal with it in any way.

He'd tried a few times to write a real letter to Elly, one where he told her about the thing with Bernard, even though he knew it would be irresponsible to tell her stuff that would make her worry. But what made it impossible to get down a draft was that nothing had really happened. Ricky dimly understood that even less happened in those letters of Elly's that he found so fascinating—but he couldn't make whatever leap it was that allowed one to impart significance to some particular span of time.

As he drove he had to remind himself not to daydream too much and to pay attention to the other cars. It wasn't that long of a drive, so he barely had enough time to cycle through all the radio stations twice before he was at Jaubert's.

He sat out in front of the bar for a while, listening to the engine click and to the soft roar of traffic. Jaubert's was a dingy little place. How had he never noticed it before? It was right out here, facing a major street. Its sign looked like it had been up for years and years, Ricky probably really had ridden or driven past it a thousand times. It was part of a tiny strip mall, whose other stores were vacant. The tall trees of Kanis Park were just down the road. Ricky had dim childhood memories of its playground, plus he'd taken Elly there not long before he'd gone to jail. She'd been the youngest kid at the skate bowl, practically a little girl. He remembered how she'd eye him almost fearfully, waiting for cues on how to act. It had made him feel proud in a manful way, taking care of her like that.

He remembered things about Elly. Now he was used to thinking of her as a grown woman, but for so many years she had been so much littler than him, and it had seemed that was the way it would always be. She'd always wanted to tag along after him, and he'd put her off, in his big-brother way. Sometimes they'd strike deals, she'd do stuff in exchange for his grown-up company. Kid stuff, mainly.

And sometimes they'd played games. Like there had been this one time when for a whole month they'd pretended that one of the neighborhood gangstas was planning to snatch Elly and have his way with her, and that Ricky was protecting her. Even though they'd been pretending they'd still believed it, like how when you're just waking up and you know you're in your bed but you're still panicked about your dream.

That was the kind of game she'd played in her letters, only she'd known how to hide the game in a grown-up way. He'd never been able to do it when he'd written back, never been able to do it in writing. Only in person, and now with Elly gone who would he play with?

There were three pick-up trucks in front of Jaubert's, and even through the tinted glass and between the slats of the opened blinds, Ricky could see people at the bar, big guys, moving around. It certainly wasn't like the place was hidden, and Ricky felt vaguely hurt that no one had ever pointed it out to him before.

He got out of the car and went in, locking his door behind him.

There were three guys hanging out at the bar, plus the bartender, and all of them looked up mildly at Ricky. They were sort of good old boys. "How you doing?" asked the bartender.

"Fine," said Ricky, and sat on a barstool and asked for a Bud. The bartender handed it to him in a glass mug and Ricky paid. After he took a sip, he got up and went to the bathroom. The guys watched him go.

The weathered wallpaper in the hall outside the bathroom had pictures of cute little bears doing acrobatics. They reminded Ricky of Care Bears. It was weird, seeing pictures like that in a bar like this. He went into the dirty men's room and made himself piss—it was easy, since he'd had that Coke at Ruby Tuesday. Then he looked at himself a long time in the spotted mirror, taking deep breaths, then went back to the bar.

He took his stool again and nodded at the bartender, who nodded back and said "Hey, there."

Ricky nodded yet again and said "Hey," and sipped at his beer. He kind of missed the fancy Sam Adams Elly had given him the other day, and the microbrewery stuff from Vino's, with its odd spices and accents.

"I haven't been in here before," said Ricky.

The bartender shrugged.

Ricky said, "I think a guy I know comes here a lot, though. This guy Ted? He has curly black hair?"

"Yeah, Ted comes around."

"He comes with that girl he's dating, I think."

"Yeah, he brought her here a couple times."

"Did they, like, get along?" asked Ricky.

"What?"

"Like, did they get along?"

"How should I know?"

Ricky turned and asked the other two guys at the bar if they knew Ted. They were having a private conversation, so Ricky had to ask them twice. One drinker said to his buddy, by way of explanation, "Ted's the one with the stuck-up bitch girlfriend."

Ricky's head was like a conch with the sea in it. "That so?" he said. "How come you say that?"

"Because it's true. Ask anybody." The drinker gestured towards the bartender. "Ask him."

The bartender shrugged and said, "Total bitch."

"That so," said Ricky. "What'd she do that was so bitchy?"

But the drinkers rolled their eyes, annoyed at Ricky for not catching on that the game wasn't fun, and returned to their conversation.

To the bartender, Ricky said, "You got any idea where I might be able to find him?"

"Why would I?"

"I'm just trying to find him. To warn him that people are out looking for him. See, somebody killed his girlfriend."

"Good," said the drinker who'd called Elly a bitch, and he and his buddy laughed. Ricky took another swallow of his beer, holding tightly onto the mug's handle.

The bartender said, "Hey now," and to Ricky, "I don't know anything about that."

"Well if you could think of anyplace he might be I would really appreciate it. Because I'd really like to see the guy."

The other guys at the bar were smirking dangerously at Ricky by now. "Why?" said the bartender. "You friends with Ted, you said?"

"Yeah, I'm friends with him. But I haven't seen him in a long time and I don't know much about his girlfriend."

"Who gives a shit?" said the drinker who hadn't spoken yet, and who seemed the drunkest. "Who cares if you 'know about' his girlfriend'?"

"Well, because somebody stabbed her to death, and the natural person for them to think of is Ted."

"Good," repeated the first drinker, and he and his buddy laughed again.

Ricky took a bigger drink from his mug and said, "I guess I just want to get hold of him to let him know that the cops're looking for him."

"The cops're looking for him, huh," said the bartender.

The drunker guy said, "Shit, I'll testify about that cunt bitch if anyone wants to ask, I'll say she had it coming."

Ricky took another swallow of his Bud and set the mug back down on the bar. "I don't guess anybody here knows where Ted's at?" he asked. "Because there're all these people looking for him, and I'd like to let him know that."

The bartender was scowling now. "Hey, man, Ted's just a guy who comes in here sometimes. His girlfriend came with him twice and one time she made a scene. Whatever happened is none of my business, and it's none of yours, so how about you change the subject and finish your beer."

As a matter of fact Ricky was draining the last of his beer as the bartender spoke, and as his reply he brought the mug smashing down on the bar, sending glass shards rocketing everywhere and leaving in his grip the handle that ended now in two spikes of broken glass. The shards hit the other guys, leaving red nicks in the faces of the guy next to him and the bartender. Just under the bartender's eye a little red spot pooled. "It's my business because it's my sister, asshole," Ricky said.

The bartender stared at him like he was crazy. "Who's your sister," he said. The shock that was thawing in enough of the area around his mouth to let him speak seemed to have not yet unfrozen in the rest of his body.

"Ted's fucking girlfriend," said Ricky.

No one said anything. The bar was quiet, except for the Garth Brooks song playing.

The two drinkers sidled glances at each other. Ricky waited for one of them to make a move, his glass handle gripped tight.

The bartender, though, relaxed his body. "Shit," he said, and brought his finger up to gingerly touch the bloody spot on his face. He looked at the little speck of blood on his fingertip, then back up at Ricky. "I didn't know she was your sister, man."

"Well, she was. Now tell me about Ted."

"I don't know where Ted is, man."

Ricky continued to hold himself ready for a brawl, as if he might need to stick someone with that broken mug. The more time passed without anyone making an aggressive move, though, the sillier he felt. Besides, the mug handle did not really end in two jagged glass spikes; they were pretty clean breaks, and the ends of the handles were almost completely flat and smooth. He said, "So tell me about when he came in with Elly."

"They just came in and had some beers, man."

Ricky waved the mug handle at him. "You better do better than that," he said.

The bartender gently chose not to notice the threat. "The first time they came in they didn't stay as long as Ted usually does. He had two beers and your sister had one. The second time she didn't even finish her first one, and as soon as Ted ordered his second she was after him to finish and go. So he yelled at her to get out and drive home if she wanted to leave so bad, and she did. Ted had to call someone to come pick him up."

"So what's all this shit about Elly being a bitch, then?"

"I don't know, man. She didn't like us, was all. She was all dressed up and she acted like my bar was too skuzzy for her. It pissed me off, that's all."

The hand holding the mug handle started to fall, but Ricky rallied his strength and hefted it up again. "She wasn't a bitch," he said.

The bartender looked at Ricky a little pityingly and held up his hands, as if agreeing to pretend that Ricky had a weapon and was some sort of threat to him. He nodded, and said, "Okay. I'm sorry."

Ricky kept glaring at him, but it became clear that the guy wasn't going to go at him with a baseball bat or shotgun, and that the other two weren't going to jump him either, so Ricky reluctantly set the broken handle down on the bar. "Okay," he said, defeated.

"Yeah." The bartender kept looking at him with that pitying look. He put his hands down, though. "Sorry about your sister, bro," he said.

"Yeah." Ricky started to walk out, but stopped and said, "You see Ted around, you tell him I'm out looking for him. Hear?"

The bartender shrugged. "Sure," he said.

Well, that was it. It was over—Ricky gave up. "All right," he said, then added, "See you later," and immediately felt like a retard. He headed slowly towards the front door. Although the bartender continued to gaze at him with that kind pity, the other two were smirking. But that didn't matter. They were assholes, but not bad enough for him to be able to do anything about it.

9.

On the drive back to her place from Ruby Tuesday, Ricky had casually asked Jesse, "So, where does Paul live?"

She'd looked at him. He hadn't been able to tell whether it was a weird look, or not. "Why?" she'd asked.

"In case he wants to talk. Or in case I do. We kind of, I don't know. Hit it off."

Regardless of whether she'd thought it a weird question, she told him where Paul lived and gave him directions there from Vino's.

Right now, though, he was headed back to his mom's place on Baseline. He was starting to feel like he'd been neglecting his duties toward her.

That feeling was compounded when he pulled up in the driveway and saw that Aunt Lenora's car wasn't there. No cop cars, either—and he had his mom's. She'd been left there alone, with no way to leave. What if she wanted to go to the funeral home and look at Elly's body?

When he opened the front door he saw an open pizza box on the floor, with four slices still in it. Crusts were scattered around the floor, Ricky imagined their crumbs sinking in among the roots of the carpet. He felt dread at the sight, even though he knew that was ridiculous. Elly was murdered. Let Mom relax about the housekeeping, for fuck's sake. But it reminded him of the bad old days, before he'd gone to jail. Like those times were leaking back in, those times of their origins, the rotten root of everything. "Mom?" he called, and stepped into the house. "Mom?" he called again, as he began to walk through the house looking for her.

He checked the kitchen. Then he checked his bedroom, but she wasn't there. She was in Elly's room. When he walked in she was on the floor on the other side of Elly's bed, with her knees drawn up and her head hanging down. He almost thought she might really be hiding, so he knocked on the door and said "Mom?" like he was just checking to see if she was there. He expected her to say "Here," or something else to give him permission to enter. She didn't, though, and Ricky stood there, awkward and undecided. She was sniffing, though, loud enough that there was no way he could pretend he hadn't heard her, so finally he came into the room. He carefully shut the door behind him.

He came and stood over her. It felt like he ought to sit beside her, but she didn't make a sign like she wanted him to so he just stood there wondering what to do. His mother shuddered lightly. At last he reached down and put his hand on her shoulder, but she jerked violently away.

He looked around the bedroom for something to talk about. The walls had been painted since he'd gone away, but even so the paint job was not new. "Wow," he said to make conversation, "I guess everything is still the way it was when Elly moved out."

His mom made a mocking noise and raised her head now, though without actually looking at him. "What the fuck're you talking about?"

"What? The room. Elly's old room, with all her old stuff still in it. You came in here to . . . like . . . remember, I guess."

"Have you even looked at this room? Does it look to you like it's just the same as when Elly lived here?"

Now that Ricky looked around the room again, he saw that his mom was right. True, her bed was still in here, and on the metal shelves lining the walls he recognized some of her old board games (or had they been the family board games?), and a few of her books, or books that seemed like they could have been hers. But almost all the space had been taken over by file cabinets, old souvenir posters advertising the neighborhood association's block parties, his exercise books, shit like that.

"Are you blind?" his mom was asking. "Can you not tell that this stuff is not hers?"

"I guess I didn't notice," he said, off-guard and confused.

"Yeah," his mom snorted, as if that wasn't exactly a big surprise. Before he could ask her what she meant by that, she'd already moved on: "When Elly moved out, she packed her shit and took it with her. Or else she got rid of it, because it was kid stuff. Do you know why that is? Do you know why she did that? Because she's a grown-up. Unlike some people, who cleared out and left all their shit overflowing all over the place and left other people to take care of it."

"What? Are you talking about me?"

"Figure it out."

"Mom, I didn't exactly want to leave the way I did."

"I know, you went to jail. What a fucking comfort."

"Mom. . . . I mean, why are you mad at me? I just came to check on you, is all. You seemed upset."

"I am upset! Jesus!"

"Okay, okay, I know. . . . I guess I just. . . . I mean, I'm upset too, Mom. Why are you mad at me?"

"I just don't see why you're so much the older one but it's still your sister who's the grown-up. Can't you even try to be like she is?"

"Like she *was*, Mom."

Now his mom looked up at him, blankly, with her wrinkled gray face. Then she turned away again and her head hung limply to the side. Looking at the blue carpet, she said, "What are you doing here, anyway."

He drove around the neighborhood a while. Once he actually started thinking about where he ought to go it seemed clear that he was going to Paul's. There were a few old friends that he'd thought he was interested in looking up, back when he was on the verge of getting released. But they had mostly never been more than time-filling friends, and they didn't fit with this context. Besides, he'd never been able to get himself really excited about seeing any of them. The only people it made sense to go looking for were Paul, Jesse, and Ted. He didn't know where Ted was, and he'd just hung out with Jesse.

He had to drive all the way to Vino's to get his bearings, then turn around and make his way to Paul's place. Paul lived in a pretty shitty apartment complex, on the third floor. Jesse had said the exterior door was never locked, and it wasn't locked now. Ricky made his way up the narrow staircase and knocked on his door, still not completely sure he'd remembered the apartment number right or even made it to the right complex. The walls were green and there was a dead mouse in one of the corners of the stairwell.

Paul opened the door. As it swung open he already had his head tilted back, as if he always assumed that whoever was knocking would be taller than him. Seeing Ricky, his eyes popped and his face lit up. "Dude!" he cried, and lurched forward to take Ricky in a bear hug, or the closest thing he could manage at his size.

Ricky could feel that Paul was trying to lift him up, so to be accommodating he raised himself on his tiptoes. After they stepped apart Paul clapped Ricky on the shoulders and said, "How you doing, man? You holding up all right?"

"Oh, yeah, you know. Okay. Considering."

As if realizing what a terrible host he was being, Paul waved his arms around and said, "Come on in, dude! The place is a mess." Ricky meekly followed Paul in.

Paul scurried ahead of Ricky and kicked a path through bags, cans and old empty boxes, then knocked junk off the loveseat to clear a space for him. Then he planted himself in a beat-up armchair that was already pretty clear, which suggested it was Paul's usual spot. He used the armrests to lift himself up by his arms as he folded his legs under him, then sat cross-legged. "So," he began, "what's up? You just came to visit?"

"Yeah. I guess."

"You need to talk about stuff?" asked Paul, and looked at Ricky so solicitously that it made him feel weird. On the one hand Paul was making this face like the gravity of the situation could not possibly be overstated, but on the other hand it didn't stop him from actually looking kind of cheerful.

Ricky didn't really want to sit around and say "I feel sad" and shit like that. Instead he said, "I was wondering about that guy Ted."

Paul looked at him. "What're you wondering about him?"

"Well, he killed my sister, they think."

Paul stared at Ricky a little longer, like he was thinking stuff over. Then he dropped his eyes and, sighing, nodded, as if Ricky had a good point. "Wow, yeah," he said.

"So you think he's the one who did it, too?"

"Well, like, or a robber."

"Nothing got taken."

"They could have broken in and then Elly came in and found them there and they just killed her, and then ran off."

"They stabbed her in the face."

"Well, what do the cops think? Do they think he did it?"

"They're looking for him. They can't find him."

"Well. I guess they would know, dude."

"Yeah, but what do you think? I mean, you know the guy."

Paul dropped the eye contact, looked around the room and sighed again. "You know, man," he said, "I always kind of tried to withhold judgment about that guy. Because of the circumstances. It was, like, me and Elly had just broken up after having dated for like years. So I had a bad feeling about him. But then I was like, Maybe I'm not being fair. Maybe I would have given Elly shit about any guy she went out with after me. Anyway, it wasn't like it was exactly okay for me to talk shit about him to her. So I kept my mouth shut."

"Kept your mouth shut about what?"

"Oh, just the feeling I had about him."

"What was the feeling?"

"Just that he was kind of intense."

Ricky scratched his head behind the ear. "I'd kind of like to find him."

"Why?"

"Just to talk to him."

"Well, he lives at 27 Clover Street, sort of towards the west side of town."

"I don't think he's just sitting around his house, the cops haven't even been able to find him."

"Either way, dude, let the police handle stuff. What can you do that they can't?"

"I just want to find him."

"Why?"

"I just sort of want to be involved."

"Look, Ted's kind of an asshole. That doesn't necessarily prove anything."

"The cops must be pretty sure he's the guy. Because otherwise they'd be questioning me. Right? Because, I mean, the day after I get released from jail for being involved in this big violent crime, my sister gets killed? And they don't even talk to me? I think that's weird."

Paul stared at him. "You want the cops to, like, question you?"

Ricky was at a loss. "It just feels weird. Like, they must be really really sure that it's this guy Ted if they're not even going to talk to me."

Paul kept staring, like he was trying to figure out what to do with him. Then he got up, waded through the trash over to Ricky's couch, knocked some trash off the neighboring cushion, and sat beside him, squeezing Ricky's knee reassuringly and putting a hand on his shoulder. "Listen, man," he said, "I know how you feel. I feel all fucked up, too. Earlier today I was going through the same stuff, I had to call Jesse and ask her to just sort of come over and hang out for a while." That must have been before her and Ricky's date. Paul rocked Ricky from side to side, using his knee and shoulder as handles. "That's the kind of thing you got to do, man. That's what'll make you feel better! Is just hanging out, just talking it over with friends. Like what you're doing now."

"Sure."

"I mean, what're you thinking of doing even if you did find Ted? Are you thinking of doing anything crazy?"

Ricky kind of squirmed, but it was like he couldn't really move that much, like Paul's hands had immobilized him. "Not *crazy*," he said.

"Hey." Paul rubbed his shoulder, soothing him. "Hey, man, listen. I understand. You feel like you got to do something. But I think you're kind of in shock, man. I think you're sort of looking for some activity, to distract yourself from all this stuff that you're probably feeling, deep down. But the truth is, there's nothing you can do. I mean, it's not like you can find Ted, if the cops can't. And it's not like it would really help, if you did find him. And then, once he got arrested, or whatever, you'd be right back where you are now. With all this grief, needing to come out."

"Okay."

"I'm serious, man. Why are you looking for Ted? Even if you could find him? You were talking yesterday about hanging out with Jesse. That's what you should be doing. She has a really healing energy. Believe me, I know. She was here earlier, like I said, and she made me feel way better." Paul gave Ricky's knee another squeeze, and added, "You could come over here, too, man, to talk. We both lost something really special yesterday. My door is, like, always open."

Ricky had his hands clasped and hanging between his legs, and he was looking at his thumbs. "I just feel like I ought to find this guy because he killed Elly."

"Well, but we don't know that though."

"Well, he beat her up then, right?"

"Well, yeah," said Paul, nodding in acquiescence, "I guess that is true." He rubbed Ricky's shoulder and the back of his neck. "But what're you going to do? You're going to get yourself in a lot of trouble if you go looking for that guy. I mean, aren't you still on parole and shit?"

Ricky was starting to get goose bumps from the way Paul was rubbing him. He stood up hurriedly. "Yeah," he said. "Like

I was saying, though. I feel like I ought to at least try to find the guy. Even just to talk to him."

Paul got up too and followed him back to the front room. He shrugged, and said, "Sure. Well, like I said, he lives at 27 Clover Street."

"Okay." Ricky was hurrying to the front door. "Well, thanks, dude."

As if he only now noticed that Ricky was leaving, Paul said in an almost surprised tone, "Can I get you anything, man? Like a beer or anything?"

"Naw. I'm going to head out."

"Do you have anyplace to go?"

"I'm just going to drive around. Talk to people, and stuff."

He was out the front door now, his left foot one step down the staircase, his right one still in front of Paul's front door. "You sure, man?" said Paul.

"Yeah. I think so."

Paul looked him up and down for a while. Then he said, "I'm worried about you, man. I wish you'd think about staying here with me a while."

"Yeah, I can't do that, sorry." Even though Paul's face hadn't changed in any recognizable way, Ricky suddenly had this feeling like he could get away if he wanted—it was like the air pressure had changed. He hurried down the stairs, calling "Bye" over his shoulder, and almost tripping over his feet and tumbling the rest of the way down.

10.

He drove around a while, aimlessly again. He didn't want to go back and hang with Paul some more. There still was no one else in town to go see except his mom, Ted, and Jesse. He didn't feel like he could handle trying to make up with his mom right now. The only place he knew to go hunting for Ted was 27 Clover Street, but it was retarded to think he might be just hanging around there. Maybe at Vino's he could ask around and get some information about the guy, but he would feel awkward walking around questioning everyone. It seemed like Jesse was his best bet. Besides, she was the one most likely to agree to hang out with him.

At her apartment, he saw that all the cars but hers were gone. Awesome. Ricky didn't feel like hanging out with a whole bunch of people.

He bounded up the crumbling concrete steps to her front door and, once he'd rung the bell, bounced from one foot to the other while he waited. He heard clumping around inside, and then Jesse opened the door, wearing the same clothes from their date, which after all had been less than two hours ago. She was taken aback to see Ricky there—she literally took a step back as her eyes got big.

"Hey," she said.

"Hey," said Ricky, still bouncing back and forth from one foot to the other, his hands shoved way down deep in his pockets. She didn't invite him in right away, so to fill the time he said, "What've you been up to?"

She turned her head away somewhat and leaned back from the waist, while still keeping her eyes locked on him. "Since

Ruby Tuesday, you mean?"

He was creeping her out, he realized. He said, "I'm sorry. I just, I can't go home. My mom doesn't want me there. And I tried going and hanging out with Paul, but, well. . . ."

Jesse made a face. "You went and hung out with Paul after we had lunch?"

"Yeah." Then: "I wasn't sure where else to go."

Jesse considered him. She softened and said, "You can come in," and stepped out of the way.

Ricky ducked his head in gratitude and went in. As he stepped through the doorway Jesse did not move completely out of the way for him but only turned and stood with her back against the doorframe, so that as he passed her the side of his body brushed against the front of hers, his bicep against the small firm cushion of her breasts inside the rough lace of her bra, the back of his hand against the denim of her jeans. His breathing got harder—was she making a pass at him? Why else had she turned like that instead of really getting out of the way, when she knew he'd have to touch her? But he told himself to play it cool.

Her voice was behind him as he entered the living room. "Sorry about the mess." He looked around. Was this a mess? He couldn't be sure. It looked the same as when he'd picked her up earlier. There were some books and magazines scattered here and there, there was the coffee table with that hubcap ashtray that was overflowing plus some CD cases with bits of weed still on them. The TV was loud, it was on a commercial right now. He said to Jesse, "It's fine to me." Then, "You smoke?"

She looked at the overflowing hubcap and said, "Nah, that's my roommates'. Doesn't really bother me, though." Then she noticed the dirty CD cases and said, "Oh, you mean weed? Sometimes. You want some?" Then her face screwed up and she added, "You really shouldn't, though, right? If you're on parole?"

"Yeah, no, you're right." Actually he really, really wanted to smoke out.

But Jesse didn't pick up on that. "Okay," she said. Then her attitude shifted, from casual to concerned. She looked at him, and said, "Now what were you saying about your mom?"

"I don't know. She doesn't want me there."

"That's crazy. Of course she does."

"But she told me to leave."

"Oh." Jesse absorbed this. "It's a hard time for her, too."

"Oh, yeah, I know. It's probably harder for her than it is for me."

Jesse was scandalized. "Don't say that! That isn't true! I can tell it isn't."

Ricky shrugged, looked off to the side somewhere. "I wasn't the greatest brother, is all."

"I'm sure you were a good brother."

"Yeah, well."

"Look, everyone makes mistakes. You probably weren't perfect. But that doesn't mean you don't have the right to, like, *grieve* her."

"Yeah, well."

"Anyway, I know you were a good brother. Because why else would Elly have come to visit you and written you all those letters?"

There were suddenly needles coming out of his pores and eyes. Looking down, he blinked and said, "Yeah, well. Elly was a really good sister."

Now that he was vulnerable, she moved in close, put her hand on his arm, and rubbed it up and down while his breathing hitched. "Huh-uh," she said. "Bullshit. She was good, but I bet she wasn't that good. I bet she wouldn't have come all the way out there, or written all those letters and letters, if there hadn't been a relationship there already. Lots of siblings would have grown apart. You must have done something to keep a hold on her."

His head was hot and swelling, like a cat in a microwave. He felt his eyes stinging and getting wet, it was like her hand rubbing up and down was milking the tears from him. "Yeah, well," he said again. "We had a...." He stopped, and then started again: "You know, Elly—she kind of had low self-esteem. . . ."

Jesse kept looking at him like it hadn't even occurred to her that he had finished; then a few seconds later she kind of shook herself and tried to rally; but only managed to say, "What?"

"You know what I mean," Ricky said, and then quickly had to bring his hand up to his eyes and nose. They started to leak, hot and slick on his hand.

"Hey," Jesse said, moving to him and wrapping her other arm around his shoulders. "Hey," she said, sounding like she was in her element now, pulling him in closer to her. She pulled his head down to the crook of her neck and put her hand on the back of his head. "It's okay," she said, "it's okay. Don't worry. Let it all out."

Ricky tried to swallow the sobs but couldn't. He sniffed hard and said something.

"What?" asked Jesse.

Ricky sniffed again and cleared his throat, and again asked, "Is there anybody else here?"

Jesse stroked the back of his head and said, "No, there's no one here. They won't be back for a long time. Don't worry about anyone coming in."

Ricky nodded, sniffed, and hooked his hands around the small of her back.

She held him tight. In his ear she murmured, "Have you even cried yet? I bet you haven't. I've had this feeling, ever since we met, like you hadn't cried but you needed to." Even before Elly got killed?, he wanted to ask, but wasn't able. "The whole time, it's like there's been this horrible pressure built up."

She rubbed him some more. "Have you cried yet?" The moist heat of his breath reflected back from her shoulder onto his mouth.

He unlocked his hands at the small of her back and spread them out, splayed the fingers and pressed his palms against her back. He moved his head, rubbing his cheek against hers. He hadn't shaved for two days and wondered if his stubble against her soft cheek hurt her. Then he moved his head back some more and positioned it so that his mouth glided onto hers. It was a very gentle kiss—they didn't use any tongue at all, not even a little, the way he and Elly had.

Ricky felt so elated that she was allowing him to kiss her that it was like a hallucination. On the other hand she wasn't being super-responsive. But he figured she was just shy.

She pulled her mouth away from his, slowly. Reluctantly, maybe. He wanted to catch her eye but her gaze had demurely slid down and to the side, and now she stepped back and turned from him as she walked away. He held onto her waist as she went, but only sort of, he didn't try to really grab her. She walked out of the living room and into the kitchen, and went behind a wall so that he couldn't see her. He didn't follow because he figured that would be rude. She called, "You want a beer?"

He cleared his throat. "Sure," he said.

She came out with an opened bottle of Bud and handed it to him, then took a step back and put her hands on her hips. She stood in front of him as if they were facing each other, but her eyes stayed too low to meet his. She didn't have a beer. He took a swallow of his, then held it towards her and said, "You want some?"

"Oh, no," she said, and shook her head. They stood there a little longer. Jesse shifted her weight from one leg to the other and said, "So."

Ricky took another swallow, a big one, and said "Yeah." Almost half his beer was already gone.

Jesse went into motion, walking fast across the room and picking up her car keys from the coffee table and shoving them into her pocket. Turning back towards Ricky but still not looking at him, she said, "You want to go out and get a coffee or something?"

"But I'm already drinking a beer," said Ricky, and this time he made himself take only a sip, and slowly, like he was savoring it.

Now she looked up at him, and thought about him for a second. She said, "We could go to a bar instead. I could be the designated driver. Or we could go to like a coffee shop and you could get a beer and I could get a coffee."

"No, that's not what I meant. I meant more, like, don't you already have beers here?"

"Yeah, but only that one. Or, well, there's one more. But then that's it."

Ricky looked at her, at a loss. He walked over, put his arms around her, pulled her close and moved his face towards hers.

She ducked her head and squirmed out of his grasp, though to be nice she did hold his hand. She gave it an encouraging squeeze.

That kind squeeze set his innards caving in on themselves. Whereas a minute ago elation had turned his blood to ether, now it was clay again, and once more his head radiated a dull sickly heat. "Sorry," he said.

Jesse shook her head. "You don't have to be sorry," she reassured him. "You didn't do anything wrong. We both just got a little carried away is all."

Doom was in the clayey air, they were hopelessly suspended in the dirty hard gelatin of time and space. But Ricky felt like he ought to try something at least, mainly out of something like duty. So he said, "I liked doing that. Liked, you know, kissing you."

Jesse nodded and kept holding his hand. "Let's just, you know, take it slow. Okay? I mean, you've been through a lot here lately. Getting out of jail, and then, I mean, you're *grieving*. And to tell the truth it's kind of a rough time for me, too. . . . I mean, it doesn't compare with what you're going through, but still. I just broke up with Paul not too long ago. And plus there's all this boring shit going on with work that I won't even tell you about. . . . But, you know. I care about you, and everything. And I want to help, and everything."

Ricky hung his head. What she said about caring about him was probably even true. That didn't make it any less humiliating.

Jesse let go of his hand, but kept standing in front of him. Now that she'd defused the whole kissing thing, leaving the apartment must have struck her as less urgent. She made no move towards the door, and even said, "Do you want to watch TV or something?"

"Yeah, sure," said Ricky, grateful and a little excited that they would at least be staying in the privacy of her home. Though part of him knew better, his malfunctioning instincts assured him that there was no way this blaring feeling within him, this urge, could possibly really not be reciprocated. It didn't make sense. The energy field was too strong and loud, the idea that it was all in his head was terrifying.

Jesse walked around looking for the remote. Ricky sat on the couch in front of the TV to wait for her. Finally she found the remote, joined him. It was just like the other day with Elly. "Do you want the remote?" asked Jesse, holding it towards him, but he shook his head. So she turned back to the screen and punched in some combination of numbers and they settled in to watch some show.

One of the weirdest things about coming home from jail was how many TV shows were foreign to Ricky now. This thing Jesse had turned it to was completely new to him—he hadn't even seen any commercials for it. Now he tried to catch up. He and Jesse sat through it silently, embarrassed during the laugh tracks.

The commercials came on and they looked at each other, grimacing in friendly desperation. Then Jesse looked back at the TV, and Ricky did too. But it was too humiliating if they didn't talk during the commercials, even. He couldn't bear the knowledge of how boring to her he was. Ricky asked Jesse what this TV show was about. "Oh, you mean you never heard of it?!" she exclaimed. She told him the name of it, even though he already knew that because they'd caught the opening credits, and then she talked about who the characters were and what they were doing with each other. That got them almost to the end of the commercial break, but then the topic ran out of steam. It would be too horrible to have to admit they couldn't even maintain a commercial break's worth of talk—then, thank

God, the show came back on, finally.

Now they were able to sit there without talking. But Ricky felt like he needed to have made some progress before the next commercial break, otherwise it would just be a repeat of before. They had to find some way to interact without having to talk to each other. During one of the laugh tracks he raised his arm and put it over her shoulders, feeling retarded and clenching himself with embarrassment—it was such a made-up, movie-style move. But Jesse didn't fight it. When he closed his fingers over her shoulder and pulled her a bit in towards him, she let herself be moved. He even felt her breathing quickening and getting deeper, just like his was. Experimentally, he caressed her upper arm. She wasn't touching him back yet, but that was okay. If she'd minded what he was doing, he figured she would have said something. And after all, she'd responded earlier, when he'd kissed her.

The commercial break seemed to come out of nowhere. He turned and looked down at Jesse. She was looking up at him, her head ducked slightly, her eyes big. Ricky leaned in, made a scooping motion with his head to come up from under her slightly down-turned face and kiss her, more fully this time: he opened his mouth and gently pried hers open with his tongue, then sent his tongue in to meet hers, which shied away.

They made out like that for two whole commercials, with just their mouths working. Once the third started Ricky was thinking that he needed to make some sort of advancement— if they weren't moving forward then once the show started back up they would just stop. He put his hand on her belly and rubbed it back and forth as he kissed her. That change of position lent itself to that of half-twisting his body and raising himself a little, so that his head was sort of pressing down on her—the added pressure felt good. Jesse accommodated herself to the shift, scooted herself underneath him, and raised her other arm some to put her hand on his side, her left hand already on his right arm. It was working! And she'd already said that her roommates weren't going to be back for hours. He raised his hand and cupped her breast. The rough feel of the bra through her shirt was more erotic than her bare breast would have been, since a bra was so different from any garment he'd ever worn.

Jesse grabbed his hand and pushed it away from her breast; "Hey," she said, voice muffled because his mouth was on hers. "Hey, let's not go too far right now."

But there was no guarantee he would ever get this chance again. More, he was practically certain that Jesse would want to stop completely, once he let her slow down. He pretended she hadn't said anything. It wouldn't count if she didn't say it twice, if she said it once it was just nerves. He tried to kiss her more passionately, really using his lip muscles and tongue, and he let go of Jesse's breast to slip his hand up under her shirt and caress the skin of her belly. Now he had equal access to her breasts and her fly.

Again Jesse surfaced, pulling her mouth away from him, and said, "I don't think this is a good idea right now."

"I have a condom," he said. He dipped his head in again, this time avoiding her mouth since she'd taken it away and he didn't want to be rude, and putting his lips behind the flap of her ear and kissing the crease, flicking at it with his tongue. She shuddered, her whole body clenched quickly and opened again with voluptuous slowness.

But she still acted like she didn't want him doing that, and pushed at his shoulders again, harder this time. "Ricky," she said, her voice getting frayed, "come on, please. Get off me."

He stopped, moved his face away from hers, because he was scared of really pissing her off. He said, "I just got out of prison," and immediately felt pathetic.

She sighed and nodded, looking rattled. "I know," she said. "But I just sort of. . . ." She trailed off. He was still pinning her—that wasn't his intention but for all practical purposes it was what he was doing. Jesse glanced at the TV, then smiled weakly and said, "Hey. The show's back on."

Ricky got the hint. "Okay," he said, and sat back up and reoriented his body towards the TV. Jesse did the same. It felt

71

like a few minutes earlier he had won a huge exhilarating victory but now he had to surrender all the territory he'd gained. He did leave his arm around her shoulder, though, and she didn't protest—that had to mean something, that she didn't mind having his arm around her. And it had definitely turned her on to make out with him, especially when he'd been kissing her behind the ear.

Pretty soon the show came to an end. There was another commercial break. After a few seconds' silence, Jesse turned her head down and to the side and said, "Well, you want to do something?"

Immediately Ricky's dick started to get hard again. "Like what?"

But Jesse only said, "Like go out and get some food, maybe."

"We just had lunch not too long ago, though."

Jesse scratched her thigh to buy herself time to think of something better. All she could come up with was, "I could eat again."

Ricky shrugged, in despair—because he still had his arm around her the motion rocked her whole body. "I don't know," he said. He knew that if he let them leave the apartment he would have sort of taken his foot out of the door, and his chances of getting Jesse to fuck him would go way down. "I could just hang out here," he added lamely.

Jesse nodded, absently. There was no telling what the nod meant. She folded her hands in her lap and fidgeted her fingers, flipping them around and rubbing them against each other and watching them. Suddenly it all seemed very sad to Ricky. She was so obviously freaked out. His slim chances of fucking her didn't seem worth making her miserable. Yet he couldn't quite muster the strength to give up on it completely, and suggest himself that they leave; the best he could manage was to kind of plaintively ask, "Well, what do you feel like doing?"

"I don't know," she said hopelessly. She sat there a few more seconds, then said, "Hang on, I might have some coupons in my room for stuff we could go do. I sort of collect shit like that."

She extricated herself from Ricky's grip and left the room. He watched her, willing her to turn and look back at him over her shoulder, but she didn't.

He sat there, waiting for her, grateful again to have the TV there to camouflage his desperation. No one would have been able to tell that he was sitting there imploding—it looked like he was just watching TV.

He listened to her rustling around in her bedroom, with the sense that he was failing a test. The idea that nothing else was going to happen between them was inconceivable. This compulsion was too blaring and blistering to be confined to his own head, it had to be out there in the universe as well, in Jesse's head too. Besides, he knew it had felt good to her when he'd kissed her on the ear. There was something else he was supposed to be doing, but he couldn't figure out what it was.

Then he suddenly remembered, like a message from above, this one scene from that movie *Blade Runner*. He and Elly had both liked it when they were kids, what with their age differences it was one of the few movies they'd watched together, so maybe it was floating around in his head for that reason. There was that one scene where the brunette woman told Harrison Ford to leave her alone, and tried to leave his apartment, and Harrison Ford blocked her, then blocked her again. Then he took her in his arms and kissed her full-on—she resisted at first but then gave in. You could tell that the brunette had actually wanted to be with him the whole time, but she'd felt sort of obligated to resist.... Maybe it wouldn't work out that way in real life, but on the other hand maybe that was exactly what Jesse was waiting for him to do. If he wound up really pissing her off then she could always just make him stop.

Still he kept sitting there a few seconds longer, frozen by stage fright. But he forced himself to get up, and walked to the door she'd gone through, then stepped through it.

Jesse was sitting at a little desk. She really was going through a bunch of coupons. She looked up at him, surprised. "Ricky?" she said. "Are you okay?" He must have looked weird.

He looked down at her. Her being seated threw him for a loop. After spending a few seconds trying to figure out what to do about it, he said, "Um, would you mind standing up?"

She kept staring at him. Then she got up, but didn't step towards him yet. "Okay," she said. "Now what?"

He started to move forward, seemed to hitch to a stop, then lurched forward again and took her in his arms and leaned forward and down and kissed her.

Jesse pushed back at his chest and slid her mouth out from under his. "Whoa," she said. "Ricky, I told you. . . ."

"I need you, though," he said.

She kept squirming. "Ricky. . . ."

He grabbed her by the arms and shook her, and held her face up very close to his, letting her see his passion: "I *need* you!" he said.

With that she sort of went limp and her eyes died out. She'd given herself over. Ricky held her in his arms and felt her strange stiff looseness and felt, for the first time maybe in years, a huge elation with no edge of fear—he'd won—she was giving herself to him, he'd done it right. He worked his mouth and tongue against hers as it stirred against him, but less forcefully than before; her tongue was like a slug that had been left in the refrigerator a long time and was numb and slow now. When he pulled her shirt up over her head, she had trouble raising her arms for him, and he had to help her, gently. He took her bra off and undid her pants, and when she was losing balance he led her to the bed and lay her down on it. He got undressed and took the condom out of his wallet and held it up and showed it to her. "Look," he said. "See? I got a condom." She looked at it, sort of nodded. He unwrapped it and invited her to watch as, straddling her, he rolled it onto his dick. Her eyes flicked down there. As he made love to her, he held her tightly, her cheeks against his palms. His fingers pressed tenderly into her temples, and the flesh in front of her earlobes. He stared hard into her eyes, willing his whole soul inside her; his lips touched hers, he shared her breath, both of them lived off the same hot fog, their eyes so close to each other that the features fractured and floated loose in each one's field of vision. He rocked himself back and forth on top of her, in and out of her, willing her to make some sound, even though he would have felt silly making noises himself; and finally she did, little moans, like she was overwhelmed with feelings, somewhere deep down and far away. Then Ricky got to a point where he had to make some noises, too. He made a bunch of them in quick succession, and then he came. Once he came he kind of collapsed onto Jesse, his sweaty forehead buried in the pillow next to her ear, his mouth slack and wet on her shoulder. Then he realized that he was probably totally crushing her, so he raised himself up on his elbows and looked down into her red wet face. "Hey," he said. "How was that? For you, I mean?"

Jesse was staring out into space. After taking a half-second to gather herself, she put her arms around him and patted his shoulder a couple times. "It was fine," she reassured him.

He was a little bit hurt that she was so lukewarm, but tried not to show it. After all, it wasn't like he didn't want her to be honest with him. If it hadn't been the greatest, well, it hadn't been the greatest. He said, "It's my first time in, like, years," then felt embarrassed by the admission. Why should he, though? She had to already know he hadn't had sex with a girl in years.

"I know," she said, and patted him on the shoulder again, then rubbed him vigorously on the same spot. He thought he heard some impatience or something in her voice, so he shut up, self-conscious, and ducked his face again into the hollow between her neck and shoulder.

They lay there like that a while. Then Jesse, sounding both annoyed and apologetic, said, "Um, you're kind of heavy. . . ?"

"Sorry!" said Ricky, and started to roll off her, but remembered in time to reach down and hold the condom against the base of his softening dick, to make sure he didn't leave it inside her, along with his cum. He peeled it the rest of the way off himself and held it up for Jesse to see. "Where should I put this?" he asked.

She looked with distaste at the wet distended rubber bag hanging from his fingers. "Um, the wastebasket?"

"Oh, yeah," he said. He almost asked her where it was but then caught himself and decided to glance around first to see if he could spot one. There was one right there, in the corner of the room. He got up and walked over and dropped the loaded condom into it. Only when he turned around and was walking back to the bed did he remember that he was naked—it felt good to be naked with another person, to be intimate like that again.

He got back in bed with Jesse. The sheets were wet and cooling, like when you wake up and realize that hours earlier you wet the bed. He gathered her up into his arms, and said, "You want to just sort of lay here a while?"

"Sure," she said.

He kissed her on the top of her head, and put his leg over her legs and pulled them in towards him too. He tenderly nuzzled her hair with his lips, then felt self-conscious again—but that was silly, he didn't need to feel that way anymore, that was the whole point. Unsure of whether it was the right thing to say, he went ahead anyway and said, "Thank you."

Jesse was silent for a few seconds. Then: "It doesn't matter," she said. "It wasn't anything."

11.

Jesse got up after a while and took a shower because she had to go to work at Vino's before too long. Only a four-hour shift. She told Ricky to feel free to leave, but he waited for her to get ready so they could depart at the same time.

He drove away, well below the speed limit. He had no idea where to go looking for Ted. Jesse and Paul were the only people who would know anything, and they knew nothing. Ricky did know what the guy looked like, because he'd seen photos. He could go driving through the hipper parts of town looking for him; he knew from Elly that Ted was sort of a hipster. The odds of spotting him were crazy small—he was no more likely to be in his usual hangouts than he was to be at his house—but Ricky felt obligated to do something.

He tried to think of where the hip neighborhoods were, besides the area around Vino's. For the moment he just drove to Vino's, wondering if he would get there at the same time as Jesse. As he approached he saw Paul walking along the otherwise deserted sidewalk, a guitar case strapped to his back. Ricky pulled over and unlocked the passenger door. Instead of hopping right into the car Paul leaned forward and stared through the window at Ricky as if he didn't recognize him. Ricky leaned over again and opened the passenger door. "Need a ride?"

Paul reached around and opened the back door, put his guitar on the backseat, then got into the passenger seat and buckled his seatbelt. "Thanks, man!" he said, "I'm just going to Vino's."

Vino's was less than a minute's drive away, so you would

have thought Paul could have just held the guitar in his lap and maybe even gone without the seatbelt. As they drove off, Ricky said, "Are you in a band?"

"Yeah," said Paul, "we're playing tonight. I'm way early, I was just going to hang out a while and have some beers first." As they went through an intersection he said, "You missed the turn there." Then, "So what are you up to?"

"Just leaving Jesse's place."

"Really? That's kind of far from here, though. . . . You hung out with her again? Twice in one day?"

"Yeah." Ricky hesitated, and then said, "We're kind of dating now."

"Really?!" exclaimed Paul, staring at him.

Ricky shrugged. "Yeah, sure. Why not?"

Paul stared at him. "No reason. Just, you know. Fast."

Ricky nodded, giving the point its due. "Yeah. I guess it *is* sort of fast. Just sort of happened, I guess."

Paul kept looking at him. "Well, that's awesome, bro," he said. "Jesse is a great girl."

"Yeah."

"Oh, hey, dude, you missed another turn you could have taken. . . ."

"Oh, sorry. . . ."

"It's cool, I'm not in a big hurry. I mean, we go on last, I'm like five hours early."

Ricky had nothing to say for a few seconds. Then he said, "I was about to go driving around looking for Ted, if you can think of anyplace he might be."

"Dude, I really think you should, you know, sort of chill out a little bit about Ted."

"Well, but he killed my sister, though."

"I know. Sorry. I guess that wasn't like a very, like, sensitive thing to say. I get why you're all fucked up about that stuff. All I mean is, you're not going to be able to find him. Unless he's hanging at his house. Did you check there?"

"If he was just hanging out at his house then the cops

would've found him."

"That's true. You know what? *Don't* check out his house."
Ricky made a left turn, starting his journey around the block
so he could head back to Vino's. "It's none of my business, but
I feel like what you're doing is putting off the whole grieving
process by taking on this whole big task thing. Like, even if
you did find Ted, what then? You'd call the police and they'd
come get him. Which is going to happen anyway, I mean even
without you, they're going to get him. And after they come to
arrest him, then what? You're going to be right back the same
place where you started, with all this grief stuff still waiting to
be done."

"If I find him then I'm not going to call the police."

"Well. Okay. I actually kind of figured that and that's part
of what worries me. I mean, you're on parole, man. Right? I
mean, you don't want to get mixed up in that kind of shit. Even
though I guess no one would blame you, since it wouldn't be like
you'd gotten into some shit with just whoever. But, still, it could
wind up fucking with you." Ricky made another turn. "I mean,
even if you did, like, track down Ted or whatever. And whether
you turned him in or whether you, you know, *whatever*—I
mean, what good would it do? Would it bring back Elly? No.
Would it make you feel better? I don't think so, dude. Not for
long. Maybe for just a few seconds."

They were in front of Vino's, so Ricky stopped the car.
Paul was still looking at him. Ricky looked back at him, and
explained, trying to be clear but not too condescending about it:
"It's sort of more like an honor thing, Paul."

Paul stared at him like he was nuts. Then he said, "Okay."
He undid his seatbelt and got out of the car, he got his guitar out
of the backseat. Before he closed the front door, he leaned down
again so as to be at eye level with Ricky and said, "Seriously,
dude. Just, let go a little. Let us help you."

Ricky shrugged. He didn't ask why Paul said "us" instead
of "me."

Paul made a face like he was kind of giving up. "Okay," he

said. "Well, thanks for the ride, dude."

"No problem."

"And, listen, if you get tired of driving around, just come back here. Me and Jesse would be glad to hang out with you."

Paul closed the door and went into Vino's. Ricky drove away.

12.

Drove away to where, though? He was afraid to go see his mom again, and Elly was dead so he couldn't go to her place. He didn't know where to find Ted. But it really would be weird if he went back and hung out with Jesse and Paul again right away.

He looked at the sidewalks to see if he could spot Ted. But he wasn't sure he would even recognize him, he'd only seen a couple photos of the guy. Curly black hair. Ricky drove to the Hillcrest neighborhood, which was another hip area, and checked for guys who looked like Ted sitting on the benches. He didn't see any. He didn't even see anyone who looked all that hip. Then, looking at Jaubert's as he passed it, he went way over to Kanis Park on the other side of town and drove through the parking lot to the skating bowl. There was nobody there. He sat in the car listening to the engine idle and looked at the branches, swaying in the wind. Through the scrim of trees he heard the steady whoosh of traffic. Fuck it, he decided, he might as well go check out Clover Street, to fill the time if for nothing else.

When Paul had given him the directions to Ted's house, Ricky had recognized each turn, and he'd expected the drive there to be like a relaxed homecoming. But again shocks kept lunging out at him. He got disoriented along the way, almost lost, but not because things had changed—it was all stuff he'd never quite known.

When he rounded the corner onto Clover, the blinking of the police lights made him flinch at first, because he assumed they were coming from inside his own head. Then the whole police car formed itself in his field of vision.

Seeing the cop cars, he slammed hard on his brakes, halting in the middle of the road with a loud squeak. What he should have done was just act natural and continue driving past, but reflexes had kicked in, or something. In the rearview mirror he saw a car coming up from behind, so he pulled over onto the curb. He didn't cut the engine but he did set the parking brake.

He sat watching, even though there wasn't much action right now: just lights, no sirens. From here he couldn't see the house's number, but he figured it was Ted's. No surprise—he'd even said that the cops would be coming around Ted's. Why should he be shocked to see them there? Maybe he was just surprised that they didn't have any better ideas. He'd only bothered to come here out of desperation. But it was kind of pathetic that the cops hadn't been able to come up with anything better, what with all their resources and shit.

There were a couple of cops standing in the yard, looking around. They looked like they were keeping an eye out for Ted. Ricky's scorn was mounting—like Ted would ever in a million years come near the house with all these cops out here. Fucking stupid retard pigs.

The front door of the house opened and some more cops came out holding a handcuffed guy by the arms. He had curly black hair, he was Ted. From this far away it was hard to see clearly, but it looked like his eyes were red and his face was wet, but also like he was scowling, or smirking even. The cops pulled him through the front yard and stuck him into the back of a police car. Then the cops got in their cars too. By now people were coming out of their houses to watch, and enough cars were slowing down or even stopping that Ricky didn't seem conspicuous after all.

The cops pulled off. Ricky sat there watching. Once they were more than a few yards away from him, he took off the parking brake and followed them. They still had their lights flashing, but they hadn't turned on the sirens and they were going at a normal speed. The three cop cars went through a stop light that was green for the first but yellow for the last two—Ricky gunned it and went through while it was red. The cops didn't seem to notice.

Ricky kept following them. He was thinking that actually he maybe could wind up following them all the way, like to the police station, or wherever. He didn't know what he would do there, but maybe they would question him, or let him sit in while they questioned Ted. He could explain that he was Elly's brother and maybe they would decide that he might have some input.

But then they did put the sirens on and started to speed up. Cars got out of their way; they wouldn't get out of Ricky's way like that. Still he followed them. He was really speeding now, but apparently none of the cops looked in their rearview mirrors and noticed the ballsy driver taking advantage of the trail they blazed. Or else they didn't care.

Finally they pulled away from him. They were just going too fast.

He took his foot off the accelerator and let the car sort of drift. When he started getting too slow to be on this busy road he got into the right lane, so as to be able to pull into one of the side streets. He didn't check to see if there was any traffic coming up behind him from back there, and as he turned into that lane someone behind him honked. When he turned into a side street he didn't bother putting on the brakes at all and the inertia shoved him into the corner of his seat.

He let the car drift along the straight empty road a little while. Fuck it. So Ted was going to jail. Ricky was glad, since the guy had killed his fucking sister. Who cared that Ricky hadn't gotten a chance to talk to him first, who cared that he hadn't brought him in? Ricky thought about going to break the news to Paul, or Jesse, and even started to map out in his head the route back to Vino's. But it would have been weird to go back there already. It would have been crazy not to tell anyone, though. He decided to go back to his mom's house. It was probably time to check on her, anyway.

13.

You could hear the TV from out in the yard. Ricky opened the front door and poked his head in gingerly; "Mom?" he called. She was sitting on the couch in front of the TV, looking at it. "Hey, Mom!" he said, louder, so she could hear him over the TV's volume.

She looked at him, kind of annoyed. "What?" she said. "I heard you the first time!"

Ricky came inside and locked the door behind him. "I just wasn't sure," he said.

"Wasn't sure about what?"

"Whether you heard me."

"I just told you I did."

"Yeah, but I wasn't sure."

"Well now you know." Ricky sat down on the couch next to her. He looked at the side of her face—she kept looking straight at the TV, even though it was a commercial break. The commercials were so loud it was hard for them to hear each other. His mom's eyes were red, her mouth was tight and wrinkly, she looked a lot older than she had the other day when he'd been released. "How are you?" he asked.

"Fine," she said.

"Really?" he said, surprised.

His mom sighed. She said, "I'm just watching some TV. To relax."

Ricky nodded. He tried to keep looking at his mom's face, but there was a beer commercial on that was kind of distracting. He said, "I was just thinking earlier about how it's like I don't know any of the shows."

His mom just looked at the screen and didn't say anything.

"Because of being in jail," he supplied.

"It's not like they didn't have TV in jail," his mom snapped.

"No, yeah, that's true," he said. He nodded. "That's true." There was an empty Family-Size Doritos bag on the floor and a couple of jumbo M & M's bags.

The show was coming back on, so they quit talking. Ricky watched it. This one didn't have any laugh tracks, it was a courtroom thing. Someone had killed somebody, they were trying to figure out who did it.

Ricky watched the show, dutifully piecing together what was going on. But sitting there just watching TV with his mom and not saying anything even though Elly was dead felt even weirder and more humiliating than quietly watching TV with Jesse even though they'd just made out had. There was an interrogation scene on the TV. He said, "So did that guy actually do it?"

"I don't know. The show's not over yet."

"Oh. . . . So you don't find out till the end. . . ."

Ricky tried to concentrate on the carpet or his shoes but his interest got sucked in again. The scene was really dramatic, he really couldn't help but wonder how it was going to end. Trying to shake off its hold on his attention, he asked his mom, "So, did the cops come around to ask anything?"

Again, his mother sighed. "Ricky, I need to relax and not think about all that. Okay? Now please just let me watch my show!"

"Oh, okay," said Ricky. He returned his attention to the TV and watched the show with his mom, being supportive. Her snapping at him had the same shock of the familiar as driving through Little Rock and recognizing the old landmarks that must have always been living in his mind, unnoticed. He remembered her old stoned and drunken freak-outs, the way she'd always clumsily tried to hide the weed from him and Elly; in the beginning Elly really had been too young to recognize what it was. This was just like that, except that it was weird because then, she'd been in her fat body, but now she was in her new thin skin-sagging one. Also, it was weird because those old freak-outs were muffled in the past, but this one was really happening now. Not that she was actually freaking out. He shouldn't overreact.

At the next commercial break he felt like he ought to try again. He said, "You know, they arrested that guy Ted."

His mom didn't say anything. He could sort of feel it that she'd heard him, though.

After a few seconds he added, "I saw them doing it, actually."

There was still a little wait. Then his mom said, "Well, that's good."

"Yeah. It is." He watched the commercial a while. It was for soap. Then he said, "Except, it's not like we know for sure he did it."

"Who else would it be?"

"A robber. Or some other ex-boyfriend. Actually, anyone could have done it." His mom didn't say anything. Ricky tried her again: "I mean, just because the cops want to decide that Ted did it, that doesn't mean *we* have to go along with it. We can make up our minds about whoever we want. . . ."

His mom interrupted him: "I don't care." She was still looking at the TV even though it was still a commercial. "Is it going to bring Elly back? No. So fuck it, then, I don't care."

"No, I know."

"I haven't been thinking about anything but this for two days, Ricky! Now can we not just drop it and let me watch TV?!"

"No, no, no, yeah, that's fine." He looked at the carpet some. "It's just that it's weird that they didn't talk to us about it or anything."

"Why would they talk to us?" his mom asked bitterly.

"Well, just, you'd think they would question us."

"Why?"

"In case we might know something."

"We don't know anything."

"But they don't know that. We *might*."

"This isn't a TV show, Ricky, it's real life. We're not going to know anything."

"No. I know."

They watched TV a while. Ricky actually wouldn't have minded just continuing to watch it. But he felt his mom sitting next to him, like a dense bomb.

He sat there for a while and didn't do anything. Then he rubbed his palms on his jeans, to dry them, then said, "All right, well, I'm going to go out for a little while."

"All right," said his mom, looking at the television.

Ricky started shifting his weight around, getting ready to stand up. "Do you need anything?"

For a few seconds his mom didn't say anything. Then, sounding very tired, she said, "I just need to be left alone, Ricky. That's all."

"No, yeah, sure." He stood up and looked down at his mom. Now, even though the show was back on, she did look back at him, her loaded vibrating eyes flickering up at his. "Goodbye, Mom," he said.

"Goodbye, Ricky," she said, a little quieter than she had been before.

In the car he thought about the people he'd dealt with these last couple days. He got a warm feeling from Jesse, though it was a tenuous, diffused warmth. It was hard to argue with his mom for not wanting him around. Elly was dead. They'd already gone ahead and arrested Ted. He thought about the weird way Paul had touched the back of his neck at Paul's apartment, about his strange affection and brightness. It struck him as disrespectful somehow.

It seemed to him that something had come to him in a dream about Paul, and he tried to remember what it had been. The information had to still be there in his head, if he concentrated he should be able to find it. He didn't believe in, like, supernatural visions and stuff; but on TV, in shows and on the news both, you sometimes heard about people subconsciously figuring stuff out, picking up on subliminal clues that they put together in, say, their sleep. The more he gnawed on the shadow of the memory, the more he realized that he had had some revelation about Paul, right after Elly had died. He couldn't remember what the dream had been—but how many things could it possibly be? Only one or two seemed like obvious choices to Ricky's imagination.

Ricky drove to Vino's. When he got there Jesse was sitting alone with a beer—she must have finished her shift. When she saw Ricky come in her eyes got big, and when he sat down with her she sort of leaned away. She didn't seem able to respond when he questioned her, and so he had to ask twice: "Do you know where Paul is?"

Jesse shrugged, not looking straight at him but not wanting to take her eyes off him, either. "Just setting up," she said. "They'll play soon."

Ricky was bouncing in the chair. He wished he hadn't sat down. "Ted's been arrested," he said.

"Oh, wow," she said, but not very excitedly.

"You aren't surprised?"

She looked at him, as if warily checking something out real quick, then immediately looked back at her beer. "Well," she said, "no, not really. Because you told me the cops were looking for him. And everybody kind of figured that maybe he did it. I mean, it's not like we know for sure he did it. But of course the police would want to at least question him."

"It just seems a little suspicious, how easy it was for the cops to find him."

"Where was he?"

"At his house."

Jesse actually laughed, which made it seem like she was in a good mood. She said, "Well, *that* doesn't sound suspicious. I mean, why wouldn't they check there?"

Ricky looked at the beer she was holding and wished he had one too, so as to have something to do with his hands. "I just have a bad feeling about it," he said.

"What kind of feeling?"

"Just, a bad one." He definitely wished he hadn't sat down. "It just feels too convenient. Like, that the first person they went looking for would be the guy who actually did it. I think they're just settling, because they're too lazy to keep, like, digging."

"But Ted used to beat her up, and he's kind of nuts. And, I mean, they must have checked for, like, physical evidence and stuff."

Getting impatient, Ricky said, "Look, I'm not saying he's *definitely* the wrong guy." Frustrated, he looked around, and said, "Look, can we get out of here?"

Jesse kept looking at her beer, or else sort of towards Ricky's forearm. "No," she said. "I'd rather just hang out here."

"Come on. What do you mean, no?"

"I just, Paul's playing later and I told him I'd watch. And I kind of want to hang out here with my friends."

"But I'm talking to you about Elly."

Jesse winced. "I know," she moaned. "I know, you're right—I really ought to be. . . . I mean, can't we just talk about it here?"

"Here? No!" Then it occurred to him that she didn't already know what he was going to say, and after that he cooled down some: "I actually sort of want to talk to you about someone. Who's here. So it would be weird to do the talking here."

"Well, I kind of need some time with my friends. I mean, we've already talked about Elly and all that."

Ricky felt pressure in his head, like it was a blood balloon being steadily filled and ready to burst. "So, what, I'm supposed to just forget about it?" he demanded. "I mean, the funeral isn't even till the day after tomorrow."

Jesse lowered her head like she was ashamed—well, Ricky thought, she *should* be ashamed. Besides, Ricky figured that was a good thing, because it would help him get her to go out to the car with him, which he needed her to do. Also it was almost like she was scared. *"Please,"* he said. *"Please."* Then his joints got loose while his muscles and throat got hard, and he started to cry a little.

"Oh," said Jesse, like she was in despair. She touched him.

"No, no, please don't cry, Ricky."

Ricky wiped his face and left his hand there to hide it, furious at Jesse for making him have to cry just to get her to come with him. "Won't you just come with me? I mean, my *sister's* dead!"

Jesse gave up. She spend a few seconds gathering strength, and looked at her beer like she was thinking of downing the whole thing, but in the end accepted that she was going to have to leave that, too. "Let's go," she said, and stood up. From the back room, where the band was, could be heard the clanking chords of the guitars as they began their sound check.

Outside the sky was turning that deep brief blue. They picked their way across the treacherous parking lot. When they got to his mom's car Ricky started to unlock the driver's side door, then remembered to be a gentleman and ran around and unlocked Jesse's first.

The car bounced them around as they left the pitted lot. They rode in silence until Jesse asked, meekly yet accusingly, "So what did you want to talk about?"

"I need to think for a minute," said Ricky, and pulled onto the freeway.

There was the crunching purr of the engine, the hum of other traffic around them, the steady noise of the madly spinning wheels on the asphalt inches below their feet, like the sound of a giant steady wave that would never crest nor fall. They passed the minor-league baseball stadium on their right, shuttered now and waiting to be demolished. Amazing, to think that it could disappear after having always been there, a piece of eternity slipping down and away into nothingness. Although Ricky supposed that actually it had only been there since the sixties.

Jesse's fingers curled around her armrest. "Um," she said. "Could we slow down?"

Ricky noticed that in fact he was going pretty fast. He did slow down. The car was humming its way across town into west Little Rock. Rising through the trees and slipping back in as they passed them were the occasional big building or shopping center. He saw that he was speeding again. But this time Jesse didn't say anything, and he didn't bother to slow down.

He pulled off the exit at the end of 6-30, following the curve too fast onto the regular road. Jesse gripped her handle again and said, "Where are we going?"

"I'm thinking."

"Okay, but where are we going?"

"I'm thinking about where to go."

"Oh."

It was all different back here now, this whole part of town had been seriously built up since he'd gone away. The road he was on had once been just a county highway, and now it was a four-lane road, the asphalt was a fresher blue, the lines had been repainted recently. The trees remained, for the moment. But whereas when he was a boy he would have believed those trees were real woods, now he knew that they were only a cosmetic wall of vegetation dividing this road from another.

He tried to weigh the wisdom of what he was going to do, then gave up. *Just take the plunge,* he advised himself. "I have to confess something," he said. "I haven't been totally honest with you."

"Oh, yeah?" said Jesse, sounding unthrilled.

"Yeah. Can I trust you with something?"

"Um, maybe if it's a really important secret you shouldn't tell anyone, though."

"Well, but I have to tell someone. I need someone to know. I told Elly. But then she. . . ." He trailed off.

There was defeated resignation in her voice when she replied: "Okay," she said. "What is it?"

"Well, I, you know, I told you that I was just the driver. For those guys, when I got sent to jail. But I guess the truth is I had more to do with it than that. I guess the truth is that I shot one of the guys, too."

"You mean you were in jail for murder?" she asked, confused, her voice trembling.

"No. But that's because the cops didn't figure it out. I told them I was only the driver. And everyone else was dead so there was nobody left to say different."

Now she sounded more confused, less trembling: "But wouldn't they have tested your hands for gunpowder?"

"Well, they did. But I washed my hands."

"But what about your clothes? Didn't it get on your clothes? And I didn't think you could just, like, wash it off with hand soap. Isn't it a bigger deal than that?"

"I guess I just got lucky," Ricky snapped. "I mean, what, you think I'm just making this shit up? Why the fuck would I do that? Do you think I'm fucking crazy?"

Jesse settled quietly against the door, hugging herself and leaning her forehead against the window. Apparently her desire to keep from riling Ricky outweighed whatever concerns she might have felt about discrepancies in his story, since she didn't pursue the topic further.

Except that after a few seconds, she did ask, "Was that what you wanted to talk about?"

"What? Oh. No. Something else, mainly."

"Well. So what else did you want to talk about?"

"Just Ted," Ricky answered, "and whether he really killed Elly. I don't know, I have a bad feeling about it. Like maybe he wasn't even the one who did it."

"But how would you know, one way or the other?"

"It's just a feeling. Like, a hunch. Haven't you ever had a hunch?"

"No."

Ricky had made a turn onto a new road cut through the woods so that now they were heading back the way they'd come. Coming up on the left he could feel a big gap in the darkening trees, and then they were alongside a huge new shopping center, totally deserted except for a couple of sleeping construction machines, no cars in the parking lot and no signs yet on the stores. Ricky turned left and sent the car down the slope of the driveway into the lot, not braking enough and so sending Jesse swinging into the side of her door. He drove to the front of the shopping center and turned left again and drove alongside it, intending to make a circuit of the whole huge parking lot. "It was just," he said, "I *saw* Ted."

"When did you see him?"

"I saw him get arrested." He looked over at her suspiciously. "Didn't I tell you that?"

"I don't think so. I don't remember for sure. I think you just told me that he'd been arrested." Weirdly, she didn't then ask him how he'd come to be there while Ted was getting arrested. "Well, if they arrested him then they must have had some evidence," she said. "Or maybe they weren't even arresting him, really, maybe they just wanted to ask him some questions about stuff."

"No, they were arresting him, they had like cuffs on him."

"Okay, well, *I* don't know," said Jesse, almost wailing, "how am *I* supposed to know? If they arrested him then probably they have fingerprints or DNA or witnesses or something."

"But no, you're not listening to me," said Ricky, and he stopped driving along the perimeter of the parking lot and veered into its interior, where he started driving in big circles, the centrifugal force pressing him into his door and pushing Jesse his way.

"I'm trying to listen," she said, her voice getting teary. "But I don't understand. I mean, you saw him. Okay! You saw him?"

"I just, I saw him, and, I mean, I *know* him! I know this guy! You know what I mean? I just get this sense, like, 'I know this guy. This guy's like me.' He's exactly like me. I had this deep, like, empathy with him all of a sudden. And I could just see in his face that he hadn't done it. You know? Do you see what I'm saying?"

"No."

"But, take somebody like Paul—I look into his face, and it's completely different."

"*Paul?*"

Ricky began putting on the brake and the car slowly came

to a stop. He put the car into park and turned to face Jesse, putting his arm around the back of the seat. "I mean, why couldn't it have been Paul?" he asked, reasonably.

"Why *could* it have been Paul?! They're totally different people! And Ted was the one who was dating her!"

"But Paul was the one she'd dumped. So he had more of a motive."

"That's crazy! You saw how Paul was the other day after Elly died. We were both there. You saw him, the way he was crying."

"People can have lots of reasons for crying," Ricky said savagely.

"Ricky. Please. You're scaring me. And I don't understand what you're saying. What is it you're saying, about Paul?"

"Just, that feeling that I got, when I looked at Ted, that feeling like I knew the guy. It's the opposite when I look at Paul. It's like, when he talks about Elly, and about Ted, it's almost like he's actually talking about something else. Like he's trying to put me off the trail. Like there's something fake."

"What are you talking about?"

"All his talk about how I should just leave all this stuff alone. How I should let the cops handle everything. It's like he doesn't want me poking around!"

"Ricky, I don't know what you're talking about."

Ricky gave up. He slumped in his seat. He was exhausted. Then he held out his arms towards Jesse and said, "Would you just hold me for a while?"

Jesse leaned back against her door. "No," she said.

Roaring filled his ears and microscopic bubbles started popping under his skin. "What?" he wailed. "I'm just asking you to hold me!"

"No, Ricky," she said. Her voice was shaky. "Take me back to Vino's, please. I want to see my friends."

He kept staring at her in disbelief and horror. "But I'm only asking you to hold me!" he protested again. "And anyway, aren't *I* your friend? Aren't I kind of like your *boy*friend?"

95

Her whole body was shaking. "No," she said, "you're not my boyfriend, we're not dating, Ricky."

"Well then why did you fuck me if we're not dating?"

Jesse was blinking faster and faster. "I wanted to help you," she said, keeping control of her voice. "I wanted to just talk to you. Because that's what you're supposed to do, is help people."

"But that's what I'm asking, is for you to help me."

"I can't help you anymore." She whimpered, and said, "I'm sorry, but I think maybe you should go to a doctor, Ricky."

He shook his head in disbelief, then, after looking out the windshield for a moment, recovered himself. He turned back to Jesse and said, "Look, just hold me for a second."

"No, Ricky!"

"God damn it!" he said, and grabbed her arm and yanked her towards him—grabbing her shoulder with his other hand, he smashed their faces together. But she broke free and slapped at him with her left hand, and even though the blows were pretty lame they shocked him enough to where he warded them off, and that meant he let go of her shoulder and she was able to scramble for the door and unlock it, and open it and try to jump out. But he still had a grip on her wrist and so she hung suspended halfway out of the car, tugging on her own arm. "Let me go!" she shouted. "Let me go!"

"No, hey, shhh," said Ricky. "Hey, listen. Just calm down. Okay?"

"Fuck you!" she shouted. "Let me go!"

"Jesse," Ricky said, very sad. He was afraid that she must be hurting her arm, pulling on it like that. "Please come back inside. I can't drive away and leave you here, there's nowhere to go."

There were tears on her face, but she wasn't struggling as hard anymore. She said, "Let me *go*."

"I will," he said, soothingly. "Just come back in the car. I'll take you back to Vino's, and I won't bother you anymore."

Now she wasn't struggling anymore at all; she was just hanging halfway out of the car by her arm. "I'm sick of all you guys," she sobbed. "I'm just so sick of all you fucking guys."

He made soft shushing noises at her, and said, "I know you are. I'm sorry. Come back in the car, Jesse. I'll take you back there, and I'll try not to bother you again."

For a little bit she kept hanging there and crying. Finally she scooted all the way back onto the seat and closed and locked the door after her, still sniffling. Maybe she'd quit fighting because her arm had finally started to hurt too much.

Now it was dark. During the drive they didn't say anything for a long while. Jesse got her sniffling under control and was quiet. She kept rubbing her wrist and elbow.

When they were almost halfway back Ricky said, "I think I just need to see him."

Jesse didn't say anything.

"I feel like, if I can look him in the face and just confront him with what I think, then one way or another I'll know. You know? Because I'll just get a sense of it."

Jesse still didn't reply.

That calm that had come over him when he'd seen how he'd scared Jesse was wearing off, and he didn't fight its leaving. Instead he let his anger build its steam back up. "I mean," he said, "because I really think that motherfucker killed my sister!"

Jesse's mouth opened like she thought she was supposed to say something, but then her jaw just hung there like she didn't know what it was.

But then, as they got closer to Vino's, she did speak, like remaining silent would make her responsible for something she didn't want to be responsible for. "So," she said, gingerly; "what're you going to do?"

Ricky didn't say anything.

"Are you going to call the cops?"

He didn't say anything.

"Not that you shouldn't, if you think that's the right thing to do. I just meant, if you didn't want to do it yourself, if you didn't feel up to it, then...."

Maybe she'd been about to make the offer out of habit,

because she was used to offering to do things, but then, when she'd gotten right up close to the words and realized what they were, she couldn't actually say them and had to stop talking for lack of anything else to say.

A few seconds went by. Then she asked, "So what're you going to do when we get to Vino's?"

Ricky didn't answer. They were only a block away, anyway.

The headlights swept a tunnel of light through the crumbled parking lot before them, illuminating Paul as he slouched by with his guitar on his back, cutting across the lot on his way home. Ricky put the parking brake on, popped open his door and hopped out of the car, hearing behind him Jesse's impotent moan.

Paul had stopped walking and was staring at him, his face slack. He looked like he was trying to think of something appropriate to say.

"Did you kill my sister?" demanded Ricky.

Paul shook his head, but not like he was denying it, more like he wanted to signal that he hadn't expected the question to be asked yet, or to be asked as if it were a vulgar yes-no kind of deal. Ricky grabbed fistfuls of Paul's T-shirt and yanked him forward, head-butting him and feeling Paul's nose break. Paul tottered backwards, Ricky pushed him and he toppled, landing on his guitar with a crunching sound. In Ricky's head the crunching sound the guitar made got mixed up with the as-yet imagined noises of Paul's body breaking, and he felt run-through with the unbearable high tension of skating so close to annihilation.

Paul was on his back like a turtle. People, still fuzzy and peripheral, were running up and yelling. He heard Jesse screaming behind him. Later he wouldn't be able to remember whether it had been his name or Paul's.

Ricky sat on Paul's stomach and pounded his face. He grabbed him by the hair and slammed the back of his head into the asphalt. People had gathered around them, but all Paul's friends seemed too pussy to try to pull Ricky off. "You killed my sister!" Ricky shouted. "You fucking killed my sister, you asshole!"

Paul was just blubbering and not even trying to fight. He croaked something through mucous and his hamburger lips.

Ricky was crying. There was a smell. He put his hands on Paul's shoulders, on either side of his neck, like he'd start choking him once he caught his breath. Behind him he heard Jesse weeping.

Paul kept trying to croak words. They could have been "I fucked up, I fucked up."

Ricky squeezed his shoulders. He said, "Me, too."

Behind him Jesse laid her long cool palm flat between his shoulder blades. It took him a while to figure out what it was.

ACKNOWLEDGMENTS

Much gratitude to my editor, Carl Robert Anderson. Thank you, Mary Sheridan. Thanks to my parents, and to my brother Chris. Muchas gracias to Mike Lindgren, not merely for the innumerable bacon chili cheeseburgers and boundless buckets of beer. To Ron Kolm, too. Nick Rowan and Emilie Lemakis graciously provided the cover image.

ABOUT THE AUTHOR

J. Boyett can be reached at jboyettjboyett@gmail.com

Made in the USA
Columbia, SC
21 November 2021

49004450R00063